# THE NEW BIZARRO AUTHOR SERIES

## PRESENTS

# FELIX AND THE SACRED THOR

## JAMES STEELE

*Enjoy your ride on the Sacred Thor!* — James Steele

Eraserhead Press
Portland, OR

# THE NEW BIZARRO AUTHOR SERIES
An Imprint of Eraserhead Press

ERASERHEAD PRESS
205 NE BRYANT
PORTLAND, OR 97211

WWW.ERASERHEADPRESS.COM

ISBN: 1-936383-23-3

Printed in the USA.

You hold in your hands now a book from the New Bizarro Author Series. Normally, Eraserhead Press publishes twelve books a year. Of those, only one or two are by new writers. The NBAS alters this dynamic, thus giving more authors of weird fiction a chance at publication.

For every book published in this series, the following will be true: This is the author's first published book. We're testing the waters to see if this author can find a readership, and whether or not you see more Eraserhead Press titles from this author is up to you.

The success of this author is in your hands. If enough copies of this book aren't sold within a year, there will be no future books from the author published by Eraserhead Press. So, if you enjoy this author's work and want to see more in print, we encourage you to help him out by writing reviews of his book, telling your friends, and giving feedback at www.bizarrocentral.com.

In any event, hope you enjoy…

—Kevin L. Donihe, Editor

## DEDICATION

This is for everyone who shopped during
the Christmas season of 2009.

I hate all of you.

*yes, you too !*

# * Sacred Sheath *

Like a predator examining the herd for the smallest and weakest to take down, Felix studied the horses in the field. He wasn't searching for the smallest or the weakest, but the one he'd been hired to help. The horse that appeared the most pent up. Four years at university had taught him how to recognize this, and he had his sights set on a black stallion in the distance.

Felix hopped the fence. He was naked, and only yards away from the main road. Cars drove by. Little kids in the back seat waved to Felix. Felix waved back. He made sure to stand up straight when seen, as these children would almost certainly pattern their lives after his own.

He walked through the field, passed several grazing horses. They raised their heads and regarded him. Felix waved to them, too. He had serviced them all at least once, but somehow they sensed now was not their time and resumed usual horsy activities.

Felix approached the black horse. It lifted its head from a small pile of hay and stared at him. Felix had never met this horse before. It was a beauty. Jet black body, black hair, huge muscles rippling just below the skin. Now *this* was a stallion. Felix felt a little guilty accepting money for the job.

He wasn't particularly famous for his skills as an Equine Stress Management Specialist. Neither were his skills unique. He'd heard the farmer's black stallion was acting a little pent up and probably needed stress management from a specialist, so Felix hopped in the unemployment line around this horse farm. He started out 98th in line, and within two hours the line had dwindled down to just him. Unusually fast. This horse must be a challenge even to the most experienced ESMS. Felix wasn't intimidated, though. He'd never met a horse he couldn't work with.

Felix was now fifty feet away. He tried to keep himself from looking too eager; he was a professional, and he had to act as such. It was difficult, but he learned how to hide his eagerness in college.

Quickly, the world darkened except for a cone of light over the horse, coming from an opening in the sky. Felix paused and looked up. Angels in heaven looked down at Felix and the stallion through this opening. Felix waved to them. The angels waved back as one.

Felix walked again.

The angels began to sing. Felix paused and listened. It took a few bars for him to recognize the song as an old Beatles tune.

Thirty feet, and the horse began to wave its tail.

The angels sang louder.

Felix drew closer. More voices joined the choir.

He slowed, took it one step at a time, feeling a little self-conscious. He wasn't used to having an audience. He'd been told heaven looked the other way whenever he used his ESM degree. Perhaps the angels forgot to pay their cable bill and needed some entertainment. Well, if the heavenly bodies wanted to watch, he'd gladly show them how it was done.

Twenty feet, and the horse seemed to know who Felix was and why he was here. It was giving him a look that said, "SERVICE ME, BITCH!"

Felix smirked back at the horse. "That's Equine SM Specialist Bitch to you."

The horse shook its head.

Felix was now ten feet away. Gradually, a hundred more voices joined the choir. Felix glanced up. Seeing this many angels at one time was humbling, but their song was encouraging. Nothing would change Felix's world, that was for sure.

He stood beside the horse, stroked its mane, felt its flanks, thighs. Big, strong horse. Felix knelt down. His hand wandered from thigh to testicles.

The light from heaven brightened.

Felix's hands wandered to the horse's sheath.

The angels started playing electric violins. The sound was shocking; he backed away from the horse. The violins stopped. The angels looked down at Felix impatiently. He leaned closer and grasped the sheath. The angels rocked out again.

The horse spread its legs a little as the angels added guitars and electric bagpipes to their orchestra. Felix rubbed faster. Bagpipes and violins kept up with his pace. Light from heaven strobed in time.

Something was different about this horse. For one, nothing had come out of its sheath. Usually, after just a few rubs, a penis would slip out and flop around, ready for Felix to perform various stress management maneuvers that could only be learned in college.

He rubbed harder. Still nothing. Felix had never had trouble finding a horse's penis before. He felt something inside the sheath, but where was it? Perhaps it was stuck, or clogged from years of non-use? This horse needed help bad.

Felix gave up coaxing it out. He crept under the horse and held the sheath at eye level. He peered inside. The angels switched on their plasma speakers and played video game soundtracks.

"Oh my God! It's full of stars!"

And it was. Felix saw the whole of the universe in this horse's sheath. Jupiter and Saturn spun by. Galaxies absorbed and destroyed each other. Red giants blew into supernovae.

Felix had a sudden, uncontrollable urge to reach in and touch creation. His hand rose. The light strobed faster. Angels sang the same note. Instruments held this note and drew it out using the sky itself as a speaker. Volume climbed as Felix's fingers approached the opening.

But he hesitated. The music and strobing stopped.

"How… How do I know I'm doing the right thing?"

The angels grumbled and blared out heavy-metal-folk-rock music.

Felix smiled. "Just checking."

He slipped his arm elbow-deep into the sheath and felt around. There was the universe. He held it in the palm of his hand. He felt the meaning of life, but it was too depressing so he shook it from his mind and forgot about it.

Felix's hand closed around something long and solid. Finally, he found it! It had been hiding in the vastness of the universe, but Felix was skilled at finding equine penises. He grasped it and brought it towards him.

His forearm emerged from the sheath. The angels rang bells and shouted in triumph and jubilation. Felix pulled out to his wrist. The angels performed *Rock Concert Movement #75: Group Sex in the Mosh Pit*. Felix pulled and pulled, and finally he fell backwards and landed on his rear, horse penis resting in his lap. It was a full two feet long and five inches across the flare.

It was green.

Felix blinked.

It was translucent, too.

He stared at it, not sure what to do. The angels were no help now; they were playing ambient "thought" music. He turned the enormous wang around, held it in his hand, felt its weight. It had a base.

"This isn't a penis! It's a sex toy!"

"Correct," said a very masculine voice above him.

The horse stepped over Felix, turned around and bowed his head to the naked man cradling the horse dildo.

"You have pulled the Thor from its Sacred Sheath. Only a pervert with the purest of hearts could achieve such a thing. The other

97 could not find it. They were not worthy. I knew you would be the one."

"I don't understand," said Felix. The angels were doing a good job with the soundtrack; they were playing suspenseful plot exposition music now. "What is it? And who are you?"

The horse smiled. "I am the Sacred Horse. Thousands of years ago, I recognized there were dangers that mankind alone was not able to stop with the weapons it forged. Humanity was in danger of falling prey to these threats, but my love extended beyond my equine brethren. Because I so loved humanity, I gave up my only begotten penis—the most powerful object in the universe—as a gift to mankind. It is the Thor! It has been resting in my Sacred Sheath, waiting for a danger great enough to summon its power. Now my weapon is yours, Felix."

He looked at it. "I'm holding your penis?"

"The physical, independent manifestation of it, yes. Obviously, a penis can't survive on its own in the physical world. To act as a standalone object therein, it becomes a sex toy."

"That's logical," said Felix. "But what do I do with your p, uh... weapon?"

The Sacred Horse shook his mane in majestic slow motion. It settled in slow motion as well.

"You will know when the time is right," said the Sacred Horse. "You have already proven yourself worthy of retrieving it. Now we shall see if you are able to handle using it."

"Use it for what? What can I do with a life-size horse dildo?"

The Sacred Horse rose on his hind legs. The angels' concert reached its climax. A million voices, two hundred thousand guitars, four thousand electric bagpipes and violins, two thousand sets of bells, a thousand drums, and one banjo reverberated through the whole of creation as the Sacred Horse ran up the beam of light to heaven.

The opening to heaven closed as the horse jumped through and the last bells played. Felix was in darkness for only a moment before the rest of the world rematerialized around him. The horses on the pasture stared at Felix.

He held the horse dildo in front of him. It was heavy and droopy. The flare was as big as his fist. The shaft was as long as his arm from wrist to shoulder. It felt like it was made of gel, but there was no odor.

So he had to prove he was worthy of using it, did he? Felix smirked.

# * Violent Little Thing *

Felix was all lubed up and ready to go. The Thor rested on the floor, pointed up at the ceiling, and Felix stood on the coffee table. The thing was so large and cumbersome, he had to go down on it from a height.

He lined himself up and got into a squat. He was a loose bitch thanks to his day job, so the flare of the dildo popped in easily. Felix squatted further, taking the shaft deep into his gut.

Suddenly, the Thor sputtered. Felix froze. Dildos normally didn't sputter. He braced himself on the coffee table and slid down a little more. The Thor compressed like a piston, sprung up and threw Felix off. He smashed against the wall and dropped to the carpet. The Thor stood upright in front of the coffee table. It pulsed and breathed.

Felix wasn't giving up yet. He drilled holes into the studs in the wall and constructed a rig to hold the toy at the level he needed. He clamped the toy's base into the rig, turned around and backed up. The dildo hung too floppy. Felix reached back and held it straight, then backed into it.

The tip popped in. The Thor compressed and pushed Felix off. Felix flew into the opposite wall. He righted himself and growled at the dildo in the rig. Felix had never met a dildo he couldn't handle, and he wasn't going to lose his pride now.

He tried sitting on it in the shower. The Thor merely threw him into the ceiling.

He tried applying lube directly to the Thor, but the Thor shook off all the lube and whacked Felix upside the head.

When he regained consciousness six hours later, he searched the net for advice. Nobody had ever heard of a life-sized horse toy, let alone one that needed to be tamed. Frustrated, Felix tried sucking on the dildo, but every time his lips went near it, the Thor smacked him across the face.

At nightfall, Felix set the Thor on the coffee table. He stared at it. It stared back with one eye. It was a violent dildo. Perhaps the Sacred Horse didn't mean "using" in the way he assumed. The damn thing was unusable as a sex toy.

But Felix had work tomorrow, so he didn't have time to try anything else. Well then, he'd just have to carry the thing around until he figured out what it was for.

# * Speedy, Amusing and Likable *

Felix had wanted to become a full-time ESMS since middle school. His guidance counselors recognized his latent attraction to horses and encouraged him to continue his education by going into that field. The more Felix explored his inner pervert, the more eager he became to use that part of himself for something good.

In past generations, such curiosities and psychological conditions were suppressed by society as immoral. But in these modern times, it was widely recognized that everyone in the world was an immoral pervert at heart. Instead of suppressing their innate talents, it was decided that people should make money off them.

Felix had been told it was the oldest and most established and secure profession in the world. Everyone said horse breeders needed the services of a qualified ESMS to keep the horses from becoming too pent up. A pent up horse was an unhappy horse, and unhappy horses didn't win races.

He'd also been told the AKC needed experienced Canine SMSes. No dogs in the world were more pent up than the pampered pooches in dog shows, and without the CSMS, each and every dog show would end as a conga-line of tied canines.

Then there was the holy grail of the SM field. The San Diego Zoo. Feline SMSes were rumored to receive hazardous duty pay for their time with the tigers and lions.

After graduation, when Felix started looking for work, he realized the horrible truth. Exactly 94% of his graduating class had gone to college to pursue their true calling as a Stress Management Specialist.

Universities around the country cranked out class after class of qualified SMSes. There were so many applicants that graduates had to line up around buildings rumored to be hiring. Every skyscraper and low rise in the city developed a line that wrapped around it at least one, all full of equally qualified SMSes waiting to take the place of someone who had just been fired and prove themselves the perfect employee.

Industry and commerce had taken full advantage of the situation and built a system around it. Legal Americans filled the niche once held by illegal immigrants, except American labor now was plentiful, disposable and skilled. This meant corporations could hire

SMSes for no pay. Profits soared, and America reclaimed its place as the world leader in manufacturing and commerce, all thanks to unemployment and education.

Felix stood proudly in these unemployment lines for years. Indeed, they were the backbone of the nation's economy, and the former students standing in them were the most patriotic people in the country. Felix didn't work for pay. He worked for the privilege of being employed, knowing that whether he worked or stood in line, he was doing his part to keep his country competitive and prosperous.

Initially, his sights had been set high. He traveled to Louisville and stood in line outside Churchill Downs in the week leading up to the Kentucky Derby, hoping to pursue his dream. The line never moved. He then stood for months outside various horse breeder farms. He got a few nibbles, and held jobs in his field for a few days at a time until he asked about getting paid. Of course, he was fired and replaced by the next kid in line, who was apparently more patriotic than Felix in that he was eager to work for nothing.

Later, Felix went to minor racetracks and stood in line there. A little luck with the bored horses in harness-racing circuits, but it wasn't nearly what he'd been trained for. In recent years, his expectations shrank with his ego, and—like every SMS was forced to do eventually—he began looking for work outside his field of expertise.

Felix landed his current job in retail two months ago. He'd been standing in line around this store for four months. He saw the mistakes everyone ahead of him made and was determined not to repeat them. The kid in front of him had sneezed at the cash register while ringing out a customer and was fired on the spot. He hadn't even been kicked out the door when a manager pulled Felix inside, threw a uniform on him and plopped him down at the return desk.

This was the best job he'd ever had, in that it actually promised to pay him for his time, provided money was left in the store's budget at the end of the year. Meantime, he was to be a "speedy, amusing and likable" employee at all times. It sounded fair to Felix. He was there for the company's sake—nay, for America's sake—not his own. Still, he resented it because he wasn't doing what he liked. Horses were far easier to please than customers, and he'd much rather use his equine skills than pretend to have people skills.

Felix stood at the customer service desk, completely absorbed in his delegated duty. Five minutes after clocking in, the manager of the clothing department had dumped an entire shopping cart on him, full of clothes to be retagged.

Out the corner of his eye, he saw a customer walking towards the counter. The customer was an old lady with skin so wrinkled her nose disappeared into the folds. Her eyes had also fallen in. Felix didn't wonder how she could see; he'd heard that post-menopausal women used their stopped biological clocks to navigate the world like the ancients used longitudinal clocks to navigate the seas.

She set her hands on the counter and leaned forward. "Do you have a pair of scissors I can borrow?"

Felix feigned eagerness to help one of his fellow creatures and stepped up to the counter. He opened the drawer, pulled out a pair of scissors and handed them to her, handle first, like his kindergarten teacher taught him.

The lady smiled, but Felix couldn't tell because the wrinkles were too thick to move. Felix began to turn around to resume retagging. The lady opened the scissors, held them up to her neck and slit her jugular. Blood flew forward and splattered on Felix's shirt. Thankfully, the store's dress code of red shirt, red pants, red shoes and red underwear was just for this reason, so it blended right in. The lady fell to the floor. Her wrinkles followed her down a few seconds later.

Felix sighed. He walked to the waist-high doorway that separated the service desk from the rest of the world and opened it.

"Felix!" cried the hidden voice of the clothing department manager. Felix looked for her, but couldn't tell where her voice was coming from. "Where are you going?!"

"A customer killed herself again. I need to clean it up."

"It can wait! Get that retagging done! Hurry! We have visitors from headquarters coming!"

"But—"

"Js-js-js-sss—just get it done!"

Felix spotted her. She was in the bra section, using it as a duck blind to keep an eye on Felix. He grunted and backed up, closing the door in front of him. He turned back to the retagging and pulled a pair of pants from it. He checked the numbers, typed them in and stuck a new tag around a beltloop. Flies from the snackbar started swarming around the body on the other side of the counter.

"Felix!"

He looked away from his delegated work at the cashier manager. She glared at him like an atom bomb with one second left on the timer. She had one. She'd shown it to everyone; it was a beeping, metallic thing buried in her abdomen. It looked more like a toaster, but she insisted it was an atomic bomb, and if anybody crossed her, she'd detonate.

"Our cashiers are backed up!" she shouted. "We have lines! I'm sending you some people to ring out."

"But I have retagging to finish."

"WE'RE IN BACKUP! RING THESE PEOPLE OUT!"

Felix held his hands up in surrender to keep her from exploding. She darted into a corner. A second later, twenty women pushing shopping carts overflowing with makeup emerged from the same corner, all reeking with the scent of impatience.

Felix set the tagging gun down and returned to the register. The first customer approached the counter. She stepped on the body of the old woman and refused to move. Felix asked her to unload her cart so he could ring her out. She stood still and crossed her arms.

"Ma'am, I can't check you out unless I scan all your makeup."

"I'm not on the clock! YOU want to charge me for these things! Don't make me do YOUR job!"

Felix walked around the counter. He began unloading her merchandise. For safety reasons, employees weren't allowed to lift more than one item at a time, so it took him exactly three hours and forty-one minutes to unload her entire cart and scan every piece of eyeliner, lipstick, nail polish, eye shadow and labia highlight.

"I want a separate bag for every item," she said after he had scanned everything.

Felix nodded and bagged every piece of makeup individually. Finally—after hours had passed—he hit *total*.

The customer felt her pockets, her breasts, her rear. She reached under her skirt and fisted herself vaginally and then anally.

"Damn," she said, pulling out. "I can't find my debit card."

"We can hold your merchandise for up to twenty-four hours if you need to run to your car."

She glared at Felix indignantly. "It's not MY fault you want to charge me!"

She bent down, grabbed the scissors from the floor, opened them and slashed her throat. Her body collapsed on top of the old lady's. The flies fluttered around it.

Felix shook his head. "I can help the next person."

The next lady walked up. Felix emptied her cart and scanned and triple-bagged every item while she stood and read a twenty-four-part manga series. When she was finished, she smiled, picked up the scissors and slashed her jugular.

Felix grunted. The smell was starting to get to him. He grabbed a dustpan and broom and walked to the door. He was about to sweep the bodies up, but the cashier manager materialized around the corner and shouted at him.

"What are you doing, Felix?! We're still in backup! I'm sending you another wave! Ring these customers!"

"But they keep killing themselves! I need to clean up or—"

"It can wait!" She went into hiding again. Another forty people lined up behind the sixty that were already there. Some had been waiting to be checked out for weeks, in spite of the calls for extra cashiers.

Felix was just about to start unloading the cart when he heard another voice.

"Felix! Buddy!" It was the manager of the general merchandise side of the store. He was pushing a line of eight shopping carts, all overflowing. "I need you to sort this reshop before the bosses arrive."

"But—! But I have all this other—!"

The manager frowned. Felix knew that look. He got on his hands and knees and dropped his pants. The manager unzipped his fly and sodomized Felix. Having been reminded of his place in the store, Felix sorted the stray merchandise back into the appropriate shopping carts for each area to put back on the shelves. These carts were already full, since the entire salesfloor staff was perpetually on backup cashier duty.

He heard a wet splatter and turned his head. Another lady had slashed her throat with the scissors. He wanted to pick them up to keep other people from using them, but, if he did that, they'd just ask every five seconds to use the scissors, and he'd have to fetch them from the drawer every time, so it was easier just to leave them out.

Felix continued sorting the products. There was a lot of makeup to put back.

"FELIX!" bellowed the cashier manager. "HELP THESE CUS-TOMERS!"

"I can't. I have to sort his reshop."

"Get your line down first!"

Felix sighed and turned around. He was about to start unloading the lady's cart for checkout when—

"FELIX!" It was the manager of the clothing section, peering at him through the bras again. "Are you done with the retagging?"

"Not yet; I have to get my line down."

The clothing manager stepped out of her cover. She was wearing nothing but bras from head to toe to better blend in with her environment. She stormed over to Felix, bent him over and sodomized him. Like all female managers, she'd had a penis installed just above her vagina to help keep employees "speedy, amusing and likable."

When she was finished, Felix stood up and began retagging the clothes. Meanwhile, two more ladies slashed their throats. The pile of bodies was above the level of the counter. Felix sprayed repellant on himself to keep the flies away.

Within two hours, another twenty women had slashed their necks waiting to be checked out. The pyramid of bloodied bodies now reached up to the ceiling and was pushing one of the foam tiles out of place. Felix wished he could clean up the mess; the flies were starting to evolve resistance to the repellant.

As Felix rang up another customer, he felt an uncontrollable desire to do his *real* job. He had been delegated other tasks for so long it was hard to remember he was hired to take returns. Just once maybe he could, and avoid being sodomized at the end of the day for not getting his job done. The return line wrapped three times around the store. He forgot about the customer he was servicing and attended to that line.

"I can help you real quick, ma'am," he said to the first lady.

She placed an overflowing shopping bag on the counter. "Hi, I don't have a receipt; it's been five years, but I bought these curtains here and I just want to return them to get cash back."

"I'm sorry, ma'am, but our return policy only goes out to two hundred days."

"But I bought these here! I paid cash! I want cash back!"

"I'm sorry—"

"Are you telling me your store doesn't stand behind its products?"

"We do, up until two hundred days, with a receipt. If you had a receipt—"

"That is the most ridiculous thing I've ever heard! Whoever heard of a limit on returns!?"

"It is this store's policy, Ma'am."

"But I set fire to these curtains just last week and they burned up! They're obviously defective and I should get my cash back!"

There was no reasoning with this woman, Felix thought. Before, he would have simply remained "speedy, amusing and likable" and calmly recited the return policy over and over until the guest left, or committed suicide. But now Felix felt energy pulsing underneath the cash register. He glanced down at the Thor resting there. It pulsed with the power of the universe, offering help. While she rambled, he casually reached under the counter and grasped the Thor at its base. In one sweeping, flawless motion, Felix pulled out the Thor, wound up and said, "I cannot process your return," and slapped her upside the head.

*THWUUUUD!*

The woman fell to the floor, unconscious. The flies mistook her for dead and swarmed her, laying eggs in her eyes.

The next lady had sixteen kids clinging to her and her shopping cart, all screaming in sixteen-part harmony.

"Hi, I bought something from your store last night. I accidentally threw the receipt away, and the product, and I expect my cash back because I'm the customer."

"I'm sorry, ma'am, but we need the product to return it."

The lady put her hands on her hips and made a noise of indignation. "This is ridiculous! This is such a HASSLE! How dare you create a HASSLE for me! This is America; we were founded on being a nation without HASSLE!"

Felix shook his head, wound the Thor up and struck.

*THWUUUUD!*

The customer fell. Felix took the next person. This was a man dressed as a woman. It was law that only women were allowed to shop, or make returns, so to stay compliant with the law of the land, this man had traded briefs for brassieres.

"Hi," he said, "I don't have a recei—"

Felix wound up. *THWUUUUD!*

The next customer stepped up. "Hi, I don't have a—"

*THWUUUUD!*

*THWUUUUD!*

*THWUUUUD!*

This was fun! Whacking customers upside the head with a horse cock was an efficient way to handle them. Why had no one thought of it before?

*THWUUUUD!*

*THWUUUUD!*

The next customer got in a few words before Felix could swing. "Hildon'thaveareceiptbutIboughtthishereandIdeservecashbackeventhoughit'sbeentwelveyears—"

*THWUUUUD!*

Suddenly, Felix felt a strong grip on his shoulders. His pants were ripped off; a small penis put him in his place. Felix resumed ringing out customers.

Five minutes later, the general merchandise manager caught him ringing out customers, bent him into the store's "speedy, amusing and likable" position and reminded him that sorting the reshop was his top priority. Felix got up and did so for three minutes while the customers waited.

He was just about to toss a bra into the clothing cart when someone jumped him from behind. Felix could tell by the penis size that it was his cashier manager, reminding him that ringing out customers was his purpose in life.

Two minutes later, the clothing manager caught him ringing out customers, sodomized him, and Felix resumed retagging the clothing. Four minutes after that, the cashier manager saw him tagging clothes, reminded him of his place, and Felix resumed ringing customers out.

The store manager clambered over the wall of bodies that now nearly blocked the entrance to the service desk.

"Felix, good news. The bosses aren't coming, so everything can wait. You should've cleaned up these bodies before they became such a mess."

Felix felt a roar rise up from his toes. "I HAVEN'T HAD—"

The store manager skied down the pile of bodies, pushed Felix to his hands and knees and reminded him of his place. Felix accepted the correction. It was all part of his development as a "speedy, amusing and likable" employee.

The store manager finished, but Felix was quickly penetrated again, this time by the manager of the clothing section.

"Don't even think about it!" she screamed. "My task is more important!"

She finished. Instantly, Felix was slammed by the store manager.

"No! Mine is! Clean up these bodies!"

"Get out of him!" the cashier manager shouted from atop the wall. "We're in backup! He's mine!"

She rolled down the wall, shoved the store manager off Felix and mounted the humble employee herself.

"Mine! Mine!"

Two minutes later, she was knocked off and replaced by someone else. The penis size told Felix that it was the general merchandise manager.

"Back off! He has reshop to sort!"

The managers fought for position over Felix. He stayed low and accepted his place in the order of things. He wanted to be "speedy, amusing and likable," so he did what he was told.

While Felix received his correction, the Thor pulsed on the floor where he'd dropped it. It seemed to call to him. *I can help. Use me. I'll show you what your real purpose in life is.*

What if he didn't have to bend over and accept his place? What if there was another way? Felix reached out and picked up the Thor. He whipped it over his shoulder. It struck the store manager on the forehead. The Thor amplified Felix's striking force ten times, and the man flew off Felix and into the back wall. He slid down into a cart of reshop and slumped there, unconscious. The flies swarmed him and laid their many eggs in his soft tissues.

The Thor pulsed and rose out of Felix's hands. It rotated, lengthened by two inches and changed color from green to yellow. Then it returned to his hands.

"All right!" Felix shouted. "Level up!"

He swung it, testing it. It felt heavier, and yet it swung easier than before. Proudly, Felix pulled his pants up and buttoned them. He stood before the remaining three managers. They were ready to charge. He held the Thor in attack stance.

Felix figured out a way to handle all of them at once. He took aim and swung. The Thor struck the cashier manager with twice the ferocity as before, and she fell to the ground.

She beeped.

Felix always knew she'd been telling the truth. He jumped, hopped up and slid across the counter. He crouched behind it and shielded his head with the Thor. The cashier manager's abdomen vibrated. Quickly, she opened the slit in her torso, exposing the metallic, toaster-like bomb. It detonated in a micro-nuclear explosion. The shockwave threw the wall of dead customers across the store. The rest of the managers and customers flew outwards with them.

Felix rose. He looked around. The customers were gone. The managers were gone. His coworkers were gone. The flies were gone. Nothing was left but a scattered field of still bodies strewn about the store. Felix smiled, threw the Thor over his shoulder and walked to the door.

# * Epic Quest *

Metallic movement behind him caught his ear. Felix stopped, one foot still raised, about to step in the sensor that would open the door. He turned his head and looked over his shoulder.

The aisles were stacked chest-high with bodies. They lay sprawled out on endcaps and shelves. Merchandise was knocked over and scattered on top of them. It didn't appear anyone was alive.

And yet there was movement. A few of the bodies wiggled. Their clothes puffed up and swirled, like cats were trapped underneath. One of the bodies in the distance wormed around until the bulge found an opening.

A toaster crawled out from the woman's blouse. It stretched its wings and rose into the air. It hovered around for a few seconds, saw Felix as the only one standing, and flew straight for him. He held the Thor like a baseball bat. The toaster beeped at Felix as it dove.

Felix swung. He connected with the toaster, sent it tumbling slots over feet into the back wall with the televisions. It detonated, and a second shockwave rippled through the store, carrying razor sharp toaster shrapnel in all directions, picking up the bodies and redistributing them like ragdolls in a hurricane. Felix knelt and stood fast against the wind. He was a bit concerned about the radiation he was absorbing, but the Thor assured him it would shield him from it.

When the wind died down, Felix gripped the Thor with two hands and stood up straight, looking around.

Bodies began to shift again. The bulges all started in the abdomen and squirmed around. Twenty toasters slipped through the pants and shirts of their human hosts and levitated.

A toaster flew up to Felix's face. It flapped there, looking him in the eye. Felix saw his reflection in its polished aluminum exterior.

The toaster beeped and clicked as another thirty bodies shifted. Wet popping sounds came from beneath the clothes; body cavities opened up. Toasters crawled out, spread their wings and rose to fill the empty spaces between the ceiling and the floor. They beeped and dive-bombed Felix as one.

Felix ducked and rolled out of the way. The swarm careened through the empty space he'd been occupying and through the glass doors. They spread out into the parking lot. People standing in the unemployment line gasped collectively.

Felix rolled upright and jumped through the broken door. He stood on the sidewalk and held the Thor against his forehead to shield his eyes from the sun. The cityscape of enormous skyscrapers and high-rise office buildings greeted him, each structure with an unemployment line wrapped multiple times around it.

The toasters were regrouping in the parking lot. Gradually, they clumped together just above the height of the cars and flapped towards Felix. He backed up a step and looked around him. The unemployed graduates cowered against the wall. The toasters would hit someone if he stayed here, but he couldn't outrun them.

Felix thought of his time trying to use the Thor as a toy. It had quite a bit of power as a piston...

Felix inverted the Thor, stood on the underside of the flare and jumped on it. The Thor pistoned and rocketed him far above the store's roof. Perfect! On the next jump, he turned around and careened over the roof. He pogo'd deeper into the city.

Traffic below him crawled by, synchronized by the red and green lights hanging over the intersections. Felix landed in the intersection and bounced onwards. Each jump took him as high as the 50th floor, then he fell all 50 floors back down to the street, or sidewalk, or park. Felix aimed his landings to send him around tall skyscrapers, choosing carefully which buildings he could leap over.

Behind him, the toasters flapped with all their might. They tried to pick up speed, but Felix took them between buildings, over some, around others. The toasters kept up like a cartoon swarm of mosquitoes. Onlookers below stopped and stared. They were instantly mugged or hit by passing cars.

Felix reached the apex of another jump, and there ahead of him was the largest and most beautiful park in the city. It was a treasured landmark, and the city took great pride in keeping it maintained. It was also closed to the public. Some had protested the logic of forbidding the public access to its own park, but the city countered with the claim that it was the best way to keep it beautiful. This made it the perfect place to do battle with a swarm of kamikaze toasters with no risk of bystander injury.

Felix landed at steeper angles to pick up the pace. The toasters filtered in from between two skyscrapers. Three jumps later, Felix landed in the middle of the park. He pulled the Thor from between his legs, turned around and faced the swarm, Thor up and ready.

The swarm closed in. Felix waited until he could see his reflection in the lead toaster. He swung. Gel connected solidly with aluminum and the toaster flew backwards. It slammed into two others, and the three exploded. They collided with other toasters and caused a chain reaction through the swarm. Dozens of nuclear explosions multiplied together. The shockwave knocked Felix off his feet and sent the swarm tumbling.

The surviving toasters slowed to a stop and wobbled. Felix got to his feet quickly and adopted an attack stance.

The toasters didn't regroup in one, massive swarm this time, but in small groups of five or ten. They beeped at him from a distance. Felix imitated beeping at them, leapt forward and swung. Solid hit. The toaster sailed straight into one of the small, waiting clusters. One explosion caused three. Three caused ten. The combined shockwaves ripped grass from the perfectly cultivated lawn.

The chain reaction totaled eighteen toasters. Felix wound up again, but the Thor arose from his hand, suspended itself in front of his face and rotated. Lightning flew from its urethra; it elongated three more inches, thickened by about another inch, and changed color to dark purple.

To show off its new level, the Thor collected a little bit of air into a tornado. A few toasters were swept up with it.

"Just in time!" Felix shouted as he grabbed the Thor. He swung it over his head, speeding up the air current. The toasters tumbled in the forming cyclone. Felix swung faster and faster. The cyclone expanded, and, before the toasters in the distance knew what was happening, they were swept up, too. They collided in the chaotic winds and detonated. The tornado spread the shockwaves out along the outer wall of the vortex, keeping Felix safe. In no time, the tornado became a fiery cauldron of burning aluminum. He kept twirling it. The explosions became louder than the wind and twice as bright as the sun. Trees were uprooted; park benches were swept up in it; delicate flowers were ripped screaming from their beds.

The tornado's fiery glow faded as soon as the last toaster exploded. Felix stopped swinging the Thor and let it rest at his side. The winds spun themselves out. The walls of the vortex fell around him. Dust, dirt, grass and trees swirled to a halt on the ground. Felix stood in the center of a vast ring of destruction. A circular scar in the manicured city park.

Felix panted. He slung the Thor over his shoulder. Though longer and heavier than ever, it was easier to wield. Perhaps he was getting used to large dildos. Catching his breath, he pondered the situation.

Suddenly, bright yellow light shone behind him. He turned around. Heaven had opened up again, and looking through the portal of light was the Sacred Horse.

"I am very pleased with you," he said. "You have proven you can handle your weapon."

"Thanks," said Felix. "I think I'm getting the hang of this."

"Indeed you are, and now you have seen the growing evil which has caused the power of the Thor to be summoned."

"Yeah… What the hell were those things?!"

"They are the evil you must fight. They may look like toasters, but are actually cleverly disguised alien kamikaze spacecraft, poised to exterminate the human race in a single swipe. Not only do they infiltrate homes, but they embed themselves in human hosts, turning unsuspecting people into kamikaze weapons."

"Oh my… Holy shit this is…"

"Fear not!" shouted the Sacred Horse. "You are now a Sacred Warrior! A Champion of Humanity! A pervert of the purest of hearts, in which has been planted the seeds of a true hero, and I mean that in the classic sense of the word! A hard-bodied stud who spits out quotable catchphrases every fourteen minutes. A patriotic, hyper-moral statue who stands for truth, justice and the American way, which logically must be the correct way! You have been chosen to wield the Thor and use it to save the human race from annihilation!"

"Uh yeah, that's me! So what do I do next?"

"Seek out and destroy the enemy, but don't let them swarm like that again. I detect this incident has gone unnoticed, and stealth is the key to victory. If the enemy knows we're onto this plan, whoever is responsible could destroy the human race at any instant."

"I understand."

"Good luck, warrior. Oh, and you'll also have to work on your preachy speech skills. All heroes make preachy speeches. They will be invaluable against tough opponents."

The Sacred Horse neighed as the portal to heaven closed. Felix stood in the ruined park and puffed out his chest with pride. A pervert of the purest of hearts. That was definitely him.

# * At Home with Bob *

Bob had spent the last twelve years waiting in the unemployment line that wrapped around the city's aquarium. Even though he was 137th in line, he felt he would be the lucky one, and would finally be able to earn money in pursuit of his true calling.

He stood there in spring, summer, fall and winter, through hailstorms, hurricanes, floods, firestorms and meteor showers. He even endured a sustenance failure, figuring no one would stand in line during an emergency that severe. He was wrong. The line didn't budge then, and it never would.

It was plain the aquarium didn't need an Ichthyic Stress Management Specialist. Broken, defeated and with nowhere else in the city that could use his valuable training, he stepped out of line and moved back home to pursue a new plan.

Now, Bob sat on the couch facing the TV. He held a cell phone tightly to his ear. He had been holding the cell phone to his ear for the last five years, determined to give himself cancer so he could get on disability.

His elderly, vegetative mother sat in her wheelchair, looking out their apartment window. She drooled. In her lap was a puddle that had been accumulating for the last eleven years. The pool was attached to an elaborate pipe system that carried the overflow to the sink, where it was recycled into municipal water. The city paid Bob's mother an insignificant fee for her contribution. A tiny school of fish had evolved in this pool. They called themselves Saliva Fish because they had evolved a means to survive in the salty brine in her lap.

Bob held the phone to his head harder, trying to speed up the process.

Bob's mother drooled.

The door burst open. Bob turned his head and leaned forward to get a better look. Every few months, one of his relatives would come to visit, and he hoped to see his sister again.

The first thing Bob saw was a purple horse penis. Then he saw a man in red shirt, shoes and pants wielding said penis like a sword.

"Who are you?" said Bob.

"SHH!" said the man in red as the dildo led him across the living room, straight to Bob's mother.

She drooled. The drop landed in the pool. The pool overflowed by exactly one drop, which fell into the pipe network and was carried into the water supply. The city deposited a penny into her bank account.

The man walked around Bob's mother, dildo aimed at her torso. The dildo was rigid and alert. It meant business. Bob pressed the phone to his scalp harder—it had become his subconscious response to stress.

"Found you!"

The man stabbed Bob's mother straight through the stomach. She choked on her drool. Her body inflated. The sound of a muffled explosion filled the air; black smoke and fire escaped from her mouth, eyes and anus. Finally, she deflated.

Bob squeezed the phone to his scalp. "That was my mother!"

"She was possessed by kamikaze aliens," said the red man. "She could've killed you at any time. I just saved your life."

"Thanks…but what about hers?"

The man in red bent down and looked at the woman's mouth. He reached into it, pulled out a hose. At the other end of it was a piece of aluminum. Bob pressed the phone tighter to his ear.

"Ah-ha! Your mother's been dead for years! The aliens maintained her salivary system to convince you she was still alive, all so you wouldn't take away their cover!"

"Oh. Um."

"No need to thank me. I labor for humanity! Carry on!"

He dashed out the door—horse dildo leading the way—and slammed it shut behind him. Bob squeezed the cell phone even tighter to his head, looking from side to side, waiting for something else to happen.

Then he felt it. Yes… Yes! One of his neurons was mutating! It was finally happening!

# * The Standout *

Sheila stood at the back of a line of 200 people. She didn't know what job she was in line for, but it hardly mattered. She hoped her Lapine Stress Management certificate would give her an edge over the other candidates, though most employers treated SM degrees with equal weight. Somehow, she had stand out.

Others were bound to have something to help with that. Perhaps in addition to an LSM degree, they went back to school and also obtained a CSM, or an ISM, or even an FSM. Sheila couldn't compete with those people, skilled with more than one animal family. Still, she had one secret weapon that might help her stand out in this crowd. She didn't quite know how it would help her get a job, but it was worth a shot.

Sheila hung her head as the line slowly dwindled. Applicants were turned down at a rate of about one every nine hours. She had been standing in the line for the better part of a month, waiting eagerly for the chance to prove herself. She had hoped the other candidates would grow tired of waiting, and she would win the job just by outlasting her competition, but apparently the other applicants all had the same idea.

After a few more months of waiting, Sheila was ten places from the front of the line and, for the first time, she saw the job for which she was applying. *Janitor*. Not what she was hoping for at all, but she had come too far to quit now.

The applicant in front presented his résumé and copies of his diplomas to the woman at the folding table. She folded them in half. In a quarter. She rolled them into a tiny ball, dipped them in ketchup and tossed them in her mouth. She chewed loudly. The résumé and diplomas screamed for mercy. The woman swallowed. The cries faded down to her stomach.

The woman digested them. Sheila could tell because the woman strained as she produced stomach acid. She broke it down rapidly, then burped. A chemist captured the escaping air in a beaker, took it to an open lab where the scientist heated it and broke it down into its composite parts. A computer powered by a fox on a treadmill analyzed the makeup of the gas and produced a detailed printout. The scientist handed the printout to the woman at the table.

She squinted at it, rolled it up and ate it. She sat still for an hour, digesting the paper, assessing the applicant's qualifications and comparing them with those who had already applied.

"I'm sorry, but we have no available positions for you at this time. Next!"

"But I have fifteen years of experience!"

"Next!"

The applicant hung his head and submitted to the verdict. The next eight applicants all went the same way.

Finally, it was Sheila's turn. She stepped up to the woman, who gestured for her to lay her qualifications on the table for analysis.

"I didn't bring my papers with me," she said.

"I beg your pardon?" said the woman behind the table.

"I am a certified LSM Specialist, and I have one thing I'm sure nobody else in this line has."

The flow chart the woman had memorized for applicant hiring had no branch for a statement like that. She was close to calling her supervisor, but Shelia lifted her shirt. Her stomach was slitted. Shelia parted the slit with one hand. The woman behind the table peered inside.

"I have a toaster."

It beeped at the woman behind the table.

"It's been there for about a year. It burrowed in me in my sleep one night, and hasn't moved since."

The woman smiled. She belched. The scientist captured it, analyzed it and handed the printout to her. She read it. She nodded.

"I believe you are the best candidate for us."

Shelia smiled, closed the slit and let her shirt fall back down over her stomach. The woman behind the counter coughed up a few wads of paper. She spread them out on the desk facing Shelia and handed her a pen. Shelia took that pen and pressed it to the page.

She felt something penetrate her. Shelia looked down. The tip and shaft of an enormous horse penis was sticking out of her stomach. She looked over her shoulder. A man wearing all red had run her through with a massive dildo.

The toaster inside her stirred. Sheila tried to slide off the dildo, but the flare was too big; she couldn't move off it. The toaster clicked and whirred. A muffled explosion rattled her ears from the inside. Sheila's body puffed out momentarily, fire and smoke spewing out her mouth and nostrils before she regained normal size.

The dildo withdrew. Chunks of aluminum fell out of the slit. She turned around and faced the man who had violated her toaster.

"Why did you do that?!"

"You were infected with a weapon of mass destruction! I used my Sacred Weapon to detonate the toaster's stage one explosives without going nuclear. I just saved your life, and the lives of everyone around you!"

"But…but…"

"I labor for humanity! You many now sleep in peace! Away I go!"

The man walked away, dildo slung over his shoulder and bobbing with his steps. Sheila turned to the woman behind the table. The papers were gone. The woman shook her head and said, "Next applicant, please."

Sheila accepted her defeat. She felt broken, hollow and violated. Anger filled in the hollow space, along with a sense that the world owed her for her failure. The only thing left to do was go to the store and return all her stuff without a receipt.

# * Kangaroo Laser *

Felix sat down on the bench and caught his breath. He was in a court-yard surrounded by three enormous skyscrapers with minor satellite buildings between them. The courtyard was pristine and minimal. Just four trees, four benches, four sidewalks.

He set the Thor next to him. It was now tie-dyed from its most recent upgrade, and it too drooped and rested. The Thor had leveled up twice since it acquired the tornado mod. Both upgrades had increased its damage infliction stat, and the more recent one had improved the Thor's efficiency as a thrusting weapon. Felix had tested it out; the Thor could penetrate flesh, bone and some metals. Perhaps a future level would allow it to penetrate any solid.

It had been an incredible week. He'd found over a hundred invaders. He figured he'd freed about sixty people, too, preventing them from becoming unwilling suicide bombers for some mysterious alien race.

While Felix sat, heaven opened in front of him and the Sacred Horse appeared. Felix waved. The horse shook his mane at him in dramatic slow motion.

"You are doing well, Felix, but your catchphrases need work."

"I know. I'm trying."

"Keep at it. Your weapon is upgrading quickly; you should upgrade, too."

"I said I was trying."

"Good. Now, I have been monitoring enemy activity, and have discovered a factory in this city that manufactures novelty toasters."

"Sounds like a perfect cover. Out in the open, looks totally legit."

"Indeed. It's downtown."

"I know where it is. I talked to a few people who said they worked for a novelty toaster company. What do you want me to do when I get there?"

"Discover who's in charge and what they're doing. If possible, learn their ultimate goal."

"Will do."

The Sacred Horse neighed, and the window to heaven closed. This life was much better than customer service. Much more rewarding. Felix was doing something for the benefit of mankind, not merely bending over and accepting his place in the chain of command.

The Thor had kept him energized, vitalized and even sanitized. Now that he wasn't holding it, he felt incredibly tired. He shut his eyes and slept.

In the middle of the night, the Thor stirred. It woke Felix up. There was an invader in the courtyard, and the Thor sensed it. Felix picked up his weapon and let it guide him to the source.

It pulled him through the crowd of midnight pedestrians, zeroed in on a man wearing a very expensive suit. Felix charged headlong for him. The man saw him coming, turned around and ran. He was a fast runner; Felix had no hope of catching up, so he held the Thor like a javelin, wound up and threw it in an arc. The Thor made minor course corrections and sailed straight through the man's upper back.

His body puffed up. The Thor contained the explosion. Smoke escaped from the man's orifices; he deflated. Felix ran to catch up with the Thor, withdrew it from the man's clothes and wiped it off. Onlookers glanced at him, then walked faster past the scene.

"Another threat to mankind eeee-liminated!"

The man wearing the suit wobbled to his feet and picked up his briefcase. He stared at Felix. Felix patted him on the shoulder.

"You don't know it, but I just saved your life."

The besuited man ran backwards, tripped over his feet, turned around and dashed for the nearest skyscraper. Felix watched him go. As a hero, he wasn't supposed to need a thank-you, or even a reward, but sometimes it would be nice to get a little recognition.

Felix sensed someone was watching. Someone...not normal. He looked up at one of the satellite buildings next to the skyscraper. A lone figure gazed down from the roof of the 20-story building. Human, definitely, and he wasn't a vessel for an invader. His cold stare made Felix uneasy. Felix stared back.

The figure atop the building stood up straight. Felix now saw that it was holding a very large dildo. He was no expert in the species, but he knew a kangaroo's penis when he saw one, even if it was double actual size. The figure aimed it at Felix. Instinctively, he rolled out of the way.

A beam of laser fire struck where he'd been standing, burning a large hole in the concrete. Felix rolled to one knee. The figure re-aimed. Felix rolled again and again, staying one step ahead of the blasts. He wondered if he could reflect the laser back at his assailant, but didn't want to risk it.

Felix had an idea. Dodging laser fire, he rolled onto the Thor and jumped on the flare and sailed up the glass façade. He landed on the roof, a hundred paces from the figure with the kangaroo.

The figure was actually a young man. Probably Felix's age. He fired his weapon. Felix ducked. The laser appeared overhead and connected with the building behind him. Glass shattered. Fires started. People inside and on the ground panicked.

The kangaroo fired another blast. Felix rolled and jumped on the flare again and soared high above the boy. Laser bolts appeared all around, none of which even came close to striking Felix. Obviously, the boy wasn't skilled at hitting moving targets coming from this angle. Felix landed three paces from the kangaroo boy, pulled the Thor from between his legs and swung it at him. Direct hit to the face. The boy screamed as he careened off the roof.

Felix ran to the edge and peered over the side. The boy tumbled down, down, down. He squeezed the base of the kangaroo toy and vanished, leaving a distorted ring of air behind him.

Felix straightened up and looked around. The bystanders, commuters and employees in the skyscrapers paid him no mind. The employees couldn't; they'd be fired for wasting company time.

He pondered the encounter for a few moments, but then realized he was wasting time. He had to find out who was in charge of this invasion. Felix pogo'd off the building and walked downtown.

# * Booth *

The security guard's name was Albert. He was long considered an outsider among his peers, as one might easily deduce from the magazine between his fingers. *Straight Sex Weekly.*

In high school, he had been teased relentlessly for only being attracted to human women. He tried to redeem himself by pointing out that he was most attracted to 12-year-olds and younger, but it didn't stop the constant bullying.

The college years earned him teasing because he chose Criminal Justice as his major. While his peers moved on to glorious careers as SMSes, he floundered in the subjects of law and truth and justice.

His guidance consolers pleaded with him to choose an in-demand career that would open the most doors in the future, but he didn't want to be an SMS. He didn't like animals at all. He wanted to be a cop. He wanted to carry a gun and walk with authority and show those bullies that, though he may be different, he was still a success.

He had waited in the unemployment lines outside the police headquarters along with three-dozen other people, but, after five years, he gave into the pressure and went back to school. He got a minor in Canine SM and returned to the lines with a new field to pursue. He spent another six years trying to get a job at various kennels and veterinary clinics. No one needed his skills.

Finally, he just stood in any line he could find, and the last one happened to be the one that wrapped around Pat's Novelty Toaster Corporation (*keeping the American kitchen quaint for nearly a quarter century*). His education in criminal justice and canine stress management was just enough to earn him an entry-level security guard post.

Now, he sat at the main gate, reading S.S.W. on yet another lonely night in front of the factory. He wasn't allowed to carry a gun, had to call his supervisor for permission to even step out of his booth, and his movements were monitored.

Years ago, management sensed its guards might be taking extra breaks when no one was watching, so, to ensure its employees weren't wasting company time, fourteen cameras were installed and aimed at the guard's booth. But to do this without spending money on equipment, management moved all fourteen cameras from the factory and placed them around the booth.

Albert had questioned the wisdom of this move, and his boss told him he would get back with him on that. Three years had passed, and, in all that time Albert had not moved from the booth. He was being watched, and the slightest mistake would mean termination. He flipped the page of the magazine.

Discreetly reading magazines was the only behavior management did not condemn. He once tried reading a good book, but his boss yelled at him for that. The official explanation was that books required too much thought, and therefore distracted a guard from his watch. Magazines, however, required little to no thought and were therefore acceptable.

He read. He looked. He flipped the page. He absorbed sustenance from the air.

He saw movement out the front window. He looked up from his magazine. A man dressed in a retail uniform ran towards the booth, an enormous...something in one hand.

Albert threw the magazine down and sat up straight. The first activity in three years! This was his chance to take action and use his valuable training! He immediately picked up the phone and called his supervisor.

The line rang.

The man approached.

The line rang three times.

The man was almost to the booth.

The line rang five times. Albert could now see that the man was carrying an enormous dildo. It looked heavy, but he wielded it like it was made of paper.

The line rang six times.

The man zoomed past the booth and disappeared behind the wall.

The line rang twenty more times. Albert continued to wait. He didn't dare give up now that his moment had come; any mistakes he made were on tape.

# * Hub *

Felix paused and looked around. The Thor scented the air for him, searching for potential threats. There was no movement or activity. He had successfully infiltrated the high-security toaster factory undetected. Felix felt very proud of himself. Customers in line often complained about their jobs while waiting to be checked out. Felix had overheard a few security guards gripe about how they were incapable of acting on their own, and needed management approval just to breathe. Given how long it would take managers to agree on something and act on it, Felix figured he'd be able to run straight through.

He crept around the building, searching for an entrance. He came to a door. Felix tried the knob. Locked. No good. Then the Thor twitched.

"What is it, boy?"

It drew him towards the keyhole.

Felix smiled. "I like your enthusiasm, but there's no way you'll fit in there."

The Thor insisted. Felix shrugged, and thrust the Thor up to the keyhole. At first, nothing happened, but then the Thor pushed harder. The metal stretched and twisted until it expanded to twenty times its original size. The lock screamed and moaned, but it had no choice. The Thor was going in, and the lock was going to take it.

The dildo punched through to the other side. Overstretched lock pieces spilled out on the floor behind the door. Felix withdrew his weapon, and the door swung inward.

"Don't have room? Make room!" Felix said.

Cautiously, he stepped inside. He looked left and right but saw no one. Holding the Thor against his chest to keep it from flopping around and knocking something over, he walked slowly along the walls, sticking to the shadows.

He wandered aimlessly through hallways and corridors. He began to doubt anything unusual was going on here, but as soon as he wondered that, he heard machinery. Machinery that sounded large and complex. He followed the noise.

Felix rounded a corner and stopped at a locked door. Behind it, the mechanical sounds were incredibly loud. He looked for a lock to pick, but this was a bioscan lock. He wasn't sure what the bioscan

35

was supposed to read. Felix lowered the Thor and stared at the lock in defeat.

Then he remembered another customer he overheard in his checkout line. A guy in a dress was trying to pick up the woman ahead of him. He told her that bioscanners once measured the iris, fingerprints, vein structure, entire palms. The man had said the iris can be painted, fingerprints can be photocopied, and vein structure on any part of the body can be imitated by a child with a paintbrush. But there was one part of the body that always remained hidden. It was always a mystery, nobody knew for sure what it looked like, only what a man claimed, and it was nearly impossible to get a close enough look to imitate it. He then asked her if she wanted to see his access key. She grabbed a pair of scissors and killed herself.

This was a Phallic Identification Security System.

Felix smiled, raised the Thor. He pressed the enormous flare against the relatively tiny hole at waist level. The Thor adjusted its size and shape in accordance with Boolean signals emitted from the computer. It sprouted new veins, bent right, then left, shrank and grew foreskin, assuming the shape the computer recognized.

A minute later, the light over the door turned green. Felix withdrew the Thor. The tip had shrunk to about an eighth of its original size, and it was so misshapen it could barely be called a penis. It was uncut, three inches long, two inches around, bent at the middle in a 90-degree angle to the left. Veins everywhere. He would hate to meet the guard who possessed access to this area.

The Thor reinflated to its scared shape, and Felix walked in, confident he had passed the toughest of security. The door shut quietly behind him. Felix stood in awe.

Before him was a labyrinth of conveyer belts and metal-bending machines that took up the entire building. Felix strained to understand the machinery through the complexity. He walked down the stairs and descended into the factory.

After wandering for a good hour, he found an area in which toasters were constructed. Felix followed the assembly line from start to finish. Aluminum sheets were cut, bent, molded and attached to aluminum casings. Those were filled with the internal guts—heating elements and locking mechanisms.

The last machines in the line apparently made the flight modules and kamikaze-class micro-nuclear reactors. All the pieces came together automatically, and completed toasters traveled along conveyer belts to the second half of the building.

The belt split in two. Half the toasters traveled to a packing area.

Actual workers stood on assembly lines and boxed the toasters, layered styrofoam around them for protection, taped the boxes up and stacked them on pallets. Felix recognized those boxes. They were the kind sold in his store, as well as thousands of others across the country. A couple workers were loading the boxes onto a freight truck. Felix ducked low and snuck past without detection.

The other half of the toasters traveled to an open window. There, they were dropped off on a ledge overlooking the city. One by one, each toaster became active, spread its wings and took off into the night. No doubt they would find some sleeping person and burrow their way into his or her abdomen.

Felix ascended the catwalk on the opposite side of the building. Light from a window overlooking the factory grabbed his attention, and he crept along the wall to it. He stopped at the window, back against the wall. He heard a phone ringing, and voices through the glass.

"He's been very committed to his post," said an old man's voice. "Hasn't moved in years, and now that there is temptation to take action, he still follows procedure."

"Are you going to give him permission to investigate?" a second, female voice said.

"Of course not," said the man. "If I do, he might start taking the initiative and try to act on his own in other matters, which is not compliant with my company's 'obedient, predictable and tedious' mission statement for employees."

Felix peeked around the corner into the room behind the glass. Sixteen people were gathered there. Temporary employees. All had their backs to Felix, watching a wall of fourteen monitors, which showed fourteen different angles of a security guard holding a telephone to his ear.

Everybody but the man in front had a clipboard in hand. Some pointed at certain monitors with their pencils and scribbled things on their papers.

"That's the kind of commitment we like to see," said a man in his seventies who was obviously in charge. "The company can use more like him."

The temps made side-glances at each other. They noticed some were writing faster than they were, and picked up the pace.

"But how can we be sure he isn't faking his performance in order to make himself look like a good employee?" asked the man rhetorically. "That's why all of you are here. The data you temps are recording will determine whether or not he remains employed by this company."

The ones who had been writing feverishly and prolifically noticed the others had caught up, and scribbled on their clipboards even faster.

"You might be wondering at what point Albert can be considered a good employee. Once he hangs up, we will analyze the data and observations you're recording. Somewhere in that information is the answer. Only the most obedient, predictable and tedious individuals can be trusted with the privilege of working for Pat's Novelty Toaster Corporation."

The man paused for a long while. The phone kept ringing. The guard didn't budge an inch. One of the women in the group had run out of room on her clipboard, and wrote numbers and long sentences on her forearm. She glanced up at the monitors, inscribed her observation of Albert from wrist to elbow.

The other temps had run out of space on their clipboards, too. They began writing on their legs, arms and faces. Some noticed they weren't writing as fast as the others, and wrote faster, harder, longer sentences and bigger numbers.

"This is industry standard," said the old man as he surveyed the monitors. "It's the first thing you need to learn as business majors. How to cut losses as much as possible, and anything less than the perfect employee can undercut your profit margin by millions over their time of employment."

The temps had run out of room on body parts they could reach, and were now brawling, stripping off each other's clothes and writing on parts of the body they could only reach on someone else. It was write, or be written on, and eventually the temps were a pile of naked bodies writing furiously on one another.

Their pencils built up enormous friction and started mini fires. The temps screamed but continued writing, determined to prove they were ideal employees.

The old man paced in front of the monitors. Behind him, the temps were all ablaze as the mini pencil fires merged into one giant fire. Still the temps wrote, taking advantage of new bone surfaces. In no time, they were nothing but scattered ashes on the floor.

"I don't hear anyone writing," the man said. "If any of you fail to write down your observations, I'm sure the unemployment line surrounding this building is full of others who will."

No answer. The man didn't notice. He kept pacing, talking to the empty room.

Felix saw his opportunity. The man was alone; he could take him easily. Felix stood before the window, raised his Thor and brought it down over the thick glass. It didn't shatter, but fell inward as a single piece.

BOOM—THUD!

Not very dramatic, but at least Felix wouldn't have to worry about getting glass in his eyes. He jumped into the room, holding the Thor with both hands. The man turned around and regarded him, stunned.

The phone kept ringing.

The man backed up, tried to run. Felix lashed the Thor at him. It smacked his back squarely and flung him to the ground—OOF!

Felix stood over the man and held the flare at his throat.

"What is this place?! Who are you?! Who do you work for?!"

The man gasped. "My name is Pat. This is my novelty toaster company, keeping the American kitchen quaint for nearly a quarter century."

"Don't mock me with mission statements! What's going on here?!"

"We make decorative, yet functional, classic American toasters. All aluminum, no plastic, just like in the days of old, to help you achieve that classic old-time ambience in any American kitchen."

"Tell me or I'll sodomize you with this!" Felix poked Pat's larynx with the Thor.

"Kid, you don't have the guts."

"I'm customer service."

"Shit! Shit! No, don't! I'll tell you anything! Just keep that thing away from me!"

"Oh, you asked for it!"

Felix shoved the Thor under the man's back and flipped him over. Pat tried to crawl away, but Felix was faster. Felix thrust. The Thor ripped through pants, tore through underwear, and, for the next five minutes, Pat was incapable of speaking, screaming, or texting.

With the Thor deep inside his gut, Pat composed himself. His voice was strained.

"All right. I'll talk."

"Good. Now, what's going on here?"

"This is their plan."

"Whose?"

"Theirs. Bunch of people. Just like you. Have weapons."

"Others like me?"

"Yes. The one in charge. Has a Ridgeback."

"What's that?"

"Dragon. Most powerful. Weapon. Ever made. This is his. Operation. The others are. His ground forces. That's all he. Told. Me."

"What planet are you from?" Felix asked.

"Planet?"

Felix twisted the Thor in Pat's gut.

"What!?" Pat screamed. "You think this. Alien invasion?"

"Isn't it?"

Pat gasped and panted. "Find the Ridgeback. It's his plan. His! I don't know more!"

The phone kept ringing.

Felix withdrew the weapon. The man panted and wheezed and was too sore to move. He would probably be too sore for the next month, but that wasn't Felix's problem.

That last move gained the Thor enough XP to level up again. It changed color from tie-dye to solid black, and Felix got the feeling it now had a projectile mod. Finally, he could confront the enemy from a distance rather than relying on melee attacks.

Felix walked to the window, climbed over it and stepped onto the catwalk. He observed the machines cranking out toasters. He watched toasters fly out the window. He observed employees loading boxes on a pallet for transport to retail establishments around the country. Perhaps around the world.

Felix saw movement amongst the machinery. A woman a little older than Felix, carrying something large. He squinted. It was a dildo shaped like a dolphin's member, except bright pink and about five times longer than it should have been. The thing swirled around like it had a mind of its own, forming a protective ring around the woman. She was examining the machines that made the nuclear cores and inserted them into the aluminum housing.

Her weapon flinched. She looked straight at Felix. She waved the dolphin weapon over her head a few times and launched fireballs from it. Felix ducked under the attacks, aimed his Thor at the woman and twisted the preputial ring. Shards of ice streaked toward her.

She grabbed her weapon with both hands and held it like a flamethrower, sweeping a solid wall of fire back and forth at Felix. Felix held his Thor with both hands as well, and erected a wall of ice in front of him. It held the fire back, and he advanced into the gap. She turned up the heat, blasting blue flames from her dolphin. Felix squeezed his horse harder and got more ice out of it.

They met on the factory floor, circled each other, fire and ice canceling out between them. The woman took a chance and swept her flame from side to side. Felix held still so he wouldn't walk straight into the flame. Fire engulfed one of the machines. Metal melted as radioactive material spilled from the cracks. Alarms sounded. Conveyer belts stopped. Toasters on the completed side of the assembly line rose into the air.

The woman halted the flame. Felix took the opportunity to charge. He rammed her, knocking her down as toasters started flying towards them. The woman crashed and rolled, but never touched the ground. She floated up, above the rising swarm and into the ductwork above. She aimed the dolphin, launched tiny balls of fire across the factory floor and flew out through the skylight.

One of the fireballs landed next to Felix. He stared at it. The Thor gave him a bad feeling, and he ran for the catwalk with the PISS lock. Felix didn't need to unlock the door from the inside, so he just threw it open.

The fireballs on the factory floor detonated in unison. Toasters were caught in the explosion, and their destruction magnified it.

Felix ran down the corridors. The massive fireball expanded behind him. He rounded the corner and found the door with the stretched lock. Bursting through it, he dashed down the courtyard and past the security booth just as flames reached the wall.

Albert was still on the phone. It wasn't ringing anymore, but it was probably a test of his resolve. If he passed it, perhaps he would be given a promotion and allowed to carry a gun!

# * Ridgeback *

The portal to heaven was an oasis of daylight in the dead of night-time. The light was blinding to Felix, and he wished they could do this audio-only for a change.

"I told you not to destroy anything yet!" said the Sacred Horse.

"I didn't! Someone else was there! A woman with a dildo just like mine!"

"That's impossible. I had but one penis to give to mankind."

"She had a dolphin that shot fire and allowed her to fly."

"That's…" For the first time since Felix met him, the Sacred Horse seemed tongue-tied.

"And I got the information you requested. The man I interrogated didn't know a lot, but I did learn there are others like me. Others wielding weapons like mine. I believe him. Before breaking into that factory, a kid with a kangaroo tried to kill me. Now a dolphin."

"Are you certain?"

"Very. I thought you said this was an alien invasion."

"It is!"

"The man didn't know anything of aliens. I didn't see any aliens in there. Nothing like that. It was just a factory. The toasters are all manmade."

"This makes no sense. Only an enormous threat to humanity could have summoned the power of the Thor. If it isn't a massive invasion, it's not large enough to merit the Thor's power."

"You're disappointed? There are many others behind this, and the one who is leading them has a Ridgeback!"

"A what?"

"A dildo molded after a dragon! Pat said it's the most powerful weapon ever made."

"Not possible," said the Sacred Horse. He still looked confused. Off center. Not the monument to confidence Felix had come to expect. "The Thor is the most powerful weapon in the world. It has to be! It's MY penis!"

Felix folded his arms. "I'm starting to think you don't know as much as you let on."

"All of this was pretty clear cut until now."

Felix waited for the Sacred Horse to speak. He didn't. He just looked down, lost in thought.

"So, if this isn't an alien invasion, what is it? And what should I do next?"

"I don't...I don't know what your next course of action should be."

"Great. Now I don't have the greatest weapon out there, others are apparently trying to destroy the world, and you don't know what I should do about it! How did you get to be a Sacred Horse while I'm down here doing all the work?!"

Now the Horse looked up and met Felix's eyes. "Do angels sing when people approach your genitalia?"

"No."

"Well, when they do, you too will earn the right to be a consultant."

Felix shrugged. "Fair enough."

"Tell you what. I'll keep monitoring what I can. If I get anything useful, I'll let you know."

"Sounds noncommittal enough to me. I'll try to locate more of these others. Maybe I can interrogate one of them, find out where the rest are."

The Sacred Horse regained his composure and said, "Good luck, warrior."

"Yeah, sure."

The Horse neighed; the window to heaven closed.

Felix sat down on the bench in the shadow of a dozen skyscrapers and sighed. The Thor relaxed with him. He was a little disappointed that aliens weren't actually involved. Felix feared he was losing interest in this hero thing.

# * iTha *

Martha was once known as "Marth" for short, but this was far too last-decade of a nickname for a teenager to endure, so she insisted on being called "Tha" (pronounced *thuhh*).

Tha sat in the chair in the middle of her room. Her digital iwalls displayed targeted commercials 24/7. There were sixteen chat windows open on this wall overlapping the commercials. She mentally brought one chat conversation to the foreground. The iwall read her thoughts and typed an appropriate response into the window. Her mind pushed *send*, brought another chat window forward, thought a response into the text field, and sent it, too.

She answered all the chat entries in accordance with proper Internet etiquette: 1) try to delay responses by at least six hours so you don't appear eager and needy. 2) finishing a conversation implies you never want to talk to that person again. 3) use emoticons every four words so your friends can understand you.

When she answered all the chat texts on this wall, Tha turned 45 degrees to the wall on her left. She brought a window forward, glanced at the text, mentally typed a single emoticon and brought up the next window. The iwalls tracked her chat text, searched for trends and changed commercial themes appropriately.

She looked at the walls, one after the other. Each had at least ten chat windows open, and each displayed sequences of commercials in the background, variations produced by different friends chatting about different topics. When all sixty chat windows had responses, she turned back to the front wall and began anew.

From the beginning, Tha's parents knew that she was part of the Digital Generation. All the signs were there: she couldn't interact with people in the flesh, she spoke in shorthand, and things she saw on a screen engaged her more than any real world stimuli.

Real world events were slow. They were mundane. By contrast, things that happened on a computer or TV screen happened fast. They were exciting, and people discussed far-reaching subjects without hindrance. Those things were more interesting; therefore they must be real. Her parents nurtured this by buying her an ibedroom.

She wanted music. The room responded by piping her favorite tunes through the ispeakers. The music was so compressed it sounded like Realplayer on 14.4, but it was the most real sound Tha had ever heard. Reality was disorganized, but digital sound was clean and orderly, therefore it must be real.

Keeping up with all her friends was hard, tiring work, and she expressed as much on her Internet journal every few days, but she was still grateful for their support. The more chat conversations she had going at once, the more she felt in touch with reality.

Tha thought she might be tired. She got off the chair, hopped in bed and closed her eyes. Old analog mattresses placed the responsibility of knowing when it was time to sleep or wake up solely on the body. But science had long ago proven that the body cannot know what is best for itself, and only a computer can make such determinations. The imattress analyzed her body chemistry. It told her she was not sleepy, and Tha got up and returned to chatting with her friends about the meaning of life and stuff.

One of the first things Tha recognized as a little girl was that people became less real when you spoke to them in person. The things they typed in chat were far deeper, more meaningful and insightful than any conversation they carried with voice and eye contact. She preferred never to see or meet her friends. Their Internet personalities were engaging and exciting. In-person meetings would only ruin her opinion of them.

Tha heard a noise that did not come from the speakers. It was a loud thud, and it sounded uncompressed. She mentally wrote an emo online journal entry about the disturbing sound. Instantly, she received 267 responses expressing sympathy and wishing her good luck making it through this troubling time. She needed the constant support to survive from minute to minute.

The noises continued. They became more violent, and now it sounded like glass was shattering, drywall being torn. Tha kept her friends updated. She was in the middle of responding to the 149th sympathetic reply when the iwall flickered. A huge hole appeared in its center, and something red tumbled out of it into her iroom.

More sounds of struggle and fighting. Tha turned 45 degrees to the left, toward another iwall, and asked it to show her what was happening. The iwall accessed the cameras installed in the corners of her bedroom and displayed a security-camera-quality image of what was right beside her.

A man wearing nothing but red clothing wrestled with something. She didn't know what it was, but the remaining three iwalls detected her confusion and preformed an Internet search.

While the iwall searched, Tha wrote a quick journal update, and received 971 responses wishing her luck in handling the crisis and saying how completely unfair it was that this was happening to her. Tha was glad everyone agreed her life was hard, and that it wasn't fair how she was being treated.

The results came back while she was reading the replies: it was a toaster. Specifically, an analog toaster made of aluminum. Very inefficient piece of technology; it ran on springs and levers and had no connection to the Internet. Tha didn't understand how the device could work at all. If it had no net connection, how did it download updates?

Tha noticed the man was swinging something at the toaster. The toaster dodged and flew around the room while the red man chased it, swinging the thing he held again and again. She didn't recognize it either, but the iwall had anticipated this and preformed a search. The results came back just seconds later: horse penis. Immediately, targeted ads for horse sex videos began playing behind the chat windows.

The man thrust the dildo, but the toaster spread its wings and flapped up and out of the way. The man swung backhanded at the toaster. It connected with a solid, metallic clank, and the analog, outdated kitchen appliance flew across the room and through the iwall Tha was watching. It left a gaping, toaster-shaped hole where the iwall had been showing a busty woman rubbing a horse's rear end. The iwall displayed 404, then flickered out. Tha turned to the rear wall, the one her ibed was against.

The toaster dove back through the hole in the dead iwall and charged the man. He grabbed the preputial ring on the horse penis, twisted it, and a blaze of ice shards flew from the tip. It punctured the toaster and sent it reeling backwards. The toaster landed on Tha's bed, beeping in panic.

The man jumped up on the bed. He was blocking Tha's view of the iwall, so she turned to the last iwall to get a better one. The man held the dildo like a sword and thrust the enormous flare directly into one of the toaster's slots.

The toaster beeped upon penetration. The man picked it up and swung it through the corner joining the two remaining iwalls. Both displayed 404s before they collapsed. The man ducked as the shockwave from a small explosion reverberated through the room. The wind blew the rear wall atop Tha's bed. Her other ibedroom iwall fell into her parent's old-fashioned analog bedroom.

The man pushed the iwall off of him and stepped down from the nonfunctioning ibed. He looked at Tha.

"Sorry about that. I'm savin' the world." He held the horse penis up to his forehead in a salute. "One toaster at a time."

Tha didn't see him. She didn't hear him. She existed in total darkness.

The man ran out of the apartment, holding the dildo high in front of him, as though it were leading the way.

Tha had the urge to write another emo journal entry, but nothing was happening. There was no music. No color. The world was gone. Should she sleep? Did she have to go to the bathroom? There was no way of knowing.

She hoped reality would return soon. She missed her friends. She needed their support now more than ever. Life was so hard.

# * Grease *

O-Mally's was the largest of all fast food restaurant chains. It boasted over 700,000 locations around the globe. Its former menu had been scientifically proven to be the tastiest, with items like triple-fried fries, deep-fried burgers, butter-dipped quadruple-fried vegetables (as a sensible alternative) and fried water. With these signature meals, it had taken over the fast food industry.

It didn't take over the entire food industry until it filled the last need of the culinary world.

These days, eating was a hassle. It took away from time that could be better spent texting, or chatting, or working. People had whined for an end to this necessity of biology, and O-Mally's answered consumer demand to maximize their convenience.

O-Mally's took inspiration from Nikola Tesla's idea of wireless electricity, and applied the principle to food service. They perfected and patented a way to skip food and its preparation, and boil down nutrition to the essence of what people were eating: grease.

Raw grease was synthesized, fortified and processed into enormous blocks of highly concentrated nutrition. These blocks were then loaded into massive reactors, where they were molecularly broken down and broadcast over the air. Customers merely had to stand in the broadcast radius, and they would receive nutrition transdermally.

The idea caught on quickly, and soon repeater stations were installed every ten blocks or so, delivering wireless sustenance to millions of people 'round the clock, every day of the year. Food could still be prepared the old fashioned way, and a limited supply of non-broadcast food was still available, but its market share was marginal, and O-Mally's owned all that, too.

As a result of their market-cornering innovation, O-Mally's became not merely a restaurant, but a utility. To reflect their newfound indispensability, O-Mally's Inc. changed its name to Comestible Broadcast Corporation. The word "grease" was lobbied as politically incorrect, and replaced with the friendlier term, "sustenance." O-Mally's restaurants were retrofitted into something akin to power plants, and became known as Comestible Repeater Stations.

Every person in the world was billed monthly for use of the service. Keeping with the company's mission of a "hassle-free sustenance experience," consumers were automatically debited, received no statement, and never knew they even received a service. To them, sustenance was like air. It didn't come from anywhere, and it had no origin. They would be a little mystified at the disappearance of money from their checking accounts every month, but it was customary in the banking industry not to allow consumers to see their account information. Things ran much more smoothly when humans did not interfere with the actions of computers.

An entire generation of kids had grown up with the CBC transparently feeding them. None had so much as suckled on a mother's tit as a baby. They didn't know bodies needed nutrition to survive. "Hunger" was merely an entry in the online encyclopedia, its article vandalized daily by nonbelievers who scoffed because it was unsourced. CBC was working to delete all records of food, eating, farming and harvesting to make sure it remained unsourced. People couldn't be permitted to remember a time when they could feed themselves, or that would mean someday the people may want to return to that time, and wouldn't need the CBC anymore.

Felix, however, knew all about the corporation from a couple people in his return line. They were complaining about their jobs, and what they said was eye-opening. Felix was sure if anyone were to plant a kamikaze toaster anywhere of importance, it would be in one of the repeaters. Maybe all of them. Take out the repeaters in any given area, and people who happened to be standing within the radius of the station would starve to death in minutes. This was why kindergarten teachers had annual drills to teach children what to do in the event of a sustenance failure, which was run in a panic out of the dead zone until they felt sustenance in the air again.

Felix crept up to the repeater station. It looked like a standard restaurant from the outside, but this was merely a reminder of the company's humbler days when food was still ingested manually.

He stopped at a locked door. The Thor pulsed. It told him there were threats inside, so his intuition had been right. He held the Thor up to the lock. The Thor stretched it easily, and Felix was inside.

He had never been inside a repeater station. Sustenance was pervasive; he probably shouldn't go too much farther without protection. But the Thor reassured him it would offer just that.

The Thor led Felix past office doors, and even past the now obsolete original restaurant area. Felix paused to marvel at this piece of history. It was now used as the repeater's break room, and was deserted at the moment.

Exposure levels were dangerous here, even so far away from the reactor core. Employees wore hybrid radiation/environmental suits to protect themselves from the highly concentrated sustenance. On their breaks, they were permitted to sit in the break room and remove their helmets for five minutes. Any longer and they would die of sustenance poisoning. The lucky ones made it to a stall and received emergency liposuction.

The Thor led Felix to the old kitchen. He rounded the corner and entered a time capsule, preserved only by inaction.

Refrigerators, microwaves, stoves—everything was as pristine as the day it was abandoned, except for the inch-thick coating of sustenance. On the counter sat the one thing that interested the Thor: an old, analog toaster.

Felix approached the toaster. It woke up, faced him and beeped. Felix raised the Thor. The toaster spread its wings and tried to fly, but its wings were heavy with sustenance. The toaster flapped like a chicken, hopping an inch off the counter and clanging back down again.

Felix swung the Thor. It made solid contact. The toaster careened across the kitchen, collided with the wall and exploded. Heat from the explosion melted sustenance off the walls and ceiling, and it flowed down in a torrent, sweeping Felix off his feet, out of the kitchen and into the hallway that led to the main reactor.

The flow solidified halfway down the hall. Felix was up to his waist in solid fat. His body absorbed it. His waistline grew an inch. His gut bloated. His arms puffed out. His butt cheeks expanded.

Felix struggled to pry himself from the saturated yellow mass. He braced himself, pushed, but his hands absorbed the fat. Even the Thor couldn't protect him from this! He had to decontaminate quickly before he suffered sustenance overexposure.

There were emergency decon showers down every hallway, complete with personal lipo units for extreme overexposure. All he had to do was walk to one, but Felix couldn't pry himself free. His body kept absorbing the fat immediately surrounding him. After a few minutes, it absorbed enough for Felix to pry himself free. His clothes were stretched to the breaking point. Even his shoes were bursting at the seams. He was fat, or, as the CBC relabeled it, "well-nourished."

A bloated, overexposed Felix arose, holding the Thor out for balance. He waddled down the hallway. It remained empty, which meant sustenance production was at capacity. Good. He wouldn't be seen. He couldn't move very quickly with all this extra nutrition in him, and he was glad the Thor at least shielded his body from airborne sustenance so he wouldn't grow even more nourished.

At the end of the hall, he came to an icon painted on the floor. It showed a stick figure under a spray of water, globs of yellow dripping off its stick body. Felix stepped into the shower and pressed a large red button at waist-level. Hot water and chemical dispersant poured from three showerheads. Felix washed his skin and clothes, and he also gave the Thor a good scrubbing.

Four needles popped out of the walls and stuck him in the sides. The lipo machines hummed, sucked out the excess sustenance, and Felix lost two hundred pounds in four minutes.

While Felix lost the weight, he thought about that toaster. It was covered in fat just like the rest of the kitchen, which meant it had probably been in use when O-Mally's was still a place where people came to eat. Clearly, the "invasion" had been in the works for a long time.

Perhaps the original plan was to have the toasters in homes, but when the CBC took over and non-broadcast food became unnecessary, the operation changed to implanting people with them. But why not simply implant the explosive micro-nuclear reactor? Why a whole toaster? It didn't make sense, but Felix hoped that soon he would find another one of those animal dildo wielders and get some answers.

A blur moved past the shower. Felix froze, fearing he may have been spotted. The Thor vibrated a warning. It was not the warning of an invader in the area. This was the same feeling Felix got when that man with the kangaroo weapon was watching him, and when the girl with the dolphin phallus was nearby.

The shower finished a moment later. So did the lipo. Felix felt clean and pure now, and so did the Thor. Felix stepped out of the shower. The dispersant caused the water to evaporate on contact with the air. Just three steps from the shower, and he was dry.

A man stood at the door at the end of the hallway. He was using a dildo to pick the lock. It looked canine; Felix saw an unmistakable knot protruding from the PISS mechanism. The Thor wanted to engage the enemy. It started leading Felix into battle, but he held the powerful weapon back, stroked it and calmed it down.

"Not yet," Felix whispered. "Watch him. Let him lead us to his objective."

The Thor twitched in anticipation. It wanted to sodomize someone again.

What door was he picking? Felix looked at the sign above.
REACTOR CORE S1

A minute later, the lock light turned green and the door swung open. The man dashed inside.

Felix bolted for the door. He held the Thor in front of him. The door closed faster and faster and slammed shut...

...on the Thor's flare. Felix sighed in relief. He pulled the door open just enough to slip through. Allowing the door to latch behind him, he jogged quietly down the concrete hall, following the sound of footsteps.

Felix stopped at a corner and peeked around. The man was picking another PISS lock.

REACTOR CORE S2

Felix stood and waited until he heard a click. He raced the closing door and caught it before it shut, without the help of the Thor this time.

The man picked the doors leading to sectors 3 and 4 as Felix trailed him. Finally, they entered sector 5, which led to the core itself, the innermost part of the repeater station. Felix followed the man down corridors. The man entered a subsection marked CONTROL. Felix peered through the window in the door.

The man was sneaking up on a group of people watching security monitors. The monitors showed workers in the core itself, wearing heavy radiation/biological suits. They carried enormous blocks of 98% concentrated sustenance. Other workers loaded the blocks into a furnace, or controlled the switches and dials that calibrated the breakdown and transmission rate.

The sustenance concentration in the core was so high it hung in the air as a solid. Workers constantly pushed chunks of yellow matter out of their way so they could move about. The visors on their suits prevented them from looking at the sustenance directly, as doing so would cause instant obesity to the point of self-destruction.

Felix had heard that CBC wanted to replace all these men with machines, but machines could not be persuaded to work in such hazardous conditions. Illegal immigrants refused to work around such high levels of concentration, too. Thankfully, the unemployment lines were full of recent graduates who would do anything for a new cardboard box to sleep under.

The people at the monitors were pointing out the actions of employees. "Number twelve paused to sneeze; make sure he gets coached on proper use of company time." "Number sixty-three requested two bathroom breaks inside of six hours; make sure that goes in his file." "Employees are wasting valuable company time and it must be stopped."

The man now stood behind one of the senior executives. He squeezed behind the knot. The canine dildo puffed up and fired a one-eighth scale clone projectile of itself. He swept back and forth, spraying the men and women with miniature canine bullets. They lodged themselves in backs and skulls; people collapsed on their faces. Monitors on the opposite side of the room cracked and shattered. Tiny canine members stuck out of the glass, pumping like bee stingers. Perhaps they contained venom?

The man lowered his tommy gun canine and observed the scene. One of the corpses moved suddenly. It turned itself over; its clothes billowed up, up, then ripped apart. A toaster crawled out of the body and hovered in the air. The man raised his weapon again, but the toaster banged him in the head and sent him crashing to the floor as the canine dildo shot a spray of projectiles up the opposite wall and across the ceiling.

The toaster dove straight for the door Felix looked through. Quickly, he jumped out of the way. The toaster flew through the glass and shot past him down the hall and around a corner. Felix bolted after the toaster. He rounded the corner. The toaster had just plowed past a high security doorway. Solid sustenance particles wafted through the opening.

Felix dashed to the broken doorway. He couldn't see inside; the air was so thick. The Thor encouraged him to follow, but Felix wasn't sure either of them could survive so much exposure. He felt himself gaining weight already.

Footsteps squeaked to a halt at the end of the hall. Felix turned. Standing at the other end was a girl, holding a weapon shaped like an elongated elephant's member. She aimed it at him.

Another set of footsteps halted. The man with the canine weapon had recovered and now stood in the hall. He seemed shocked at the sight of Felix and the girl. She turned, regarded him, and looked shocked, too.

Then, all three transferred their shock into rage. Felix and the canine both aimed their weapons at the girl. Her weapon split in two, and the tips of the elephant penis hovered on either side of her, aimed at Felix and the canine boy.

There was an explosion inside the core. Felix dove out of the way just as a geyser of 87% concentrated sustenance sprayed from the open doorway. It coated the walls and built up an inch per second. The excess consolidated into globules the size of marbles and hung in the air like picture frames.

The girl took advantage of the distraction and sent the whip in two directions at once. The tips wrapped around both the man and Felix and dragged them towards each other. Felix and the other man screamed. They smashed together. The man slumped unconscious and dropped his weapon, but Felix had used the Thor to cushion the impact.

The girl guided Felix and the boy to the thick jet of grease. Felix swung the Thor around, twisted the preputial ring and fired ice shards at the door. At first, they melted instantly, but Felix turned down the Thor's heat. The shards came out thicker and mightier and stuck to the side of the door.

The Thor formed a wall of glacial ice six feet thick and sealed the opening. The girl's weapon still brought him into the thick atmosphere of solid sustenance, but the Thor could protect him from that. He whipped and beat the particles out of the way, making room for himself.

The girl realized she had been thwarted, and wound up to smash Felix against the floor. Felix turned the Thor on the coil wrapped around his waist. He sprayed it with ice. The tentacle froze instantly and snapped off. Felix fell. He aimed the Thor straight down. It pistoned and bounced him up.

Panting, Felix stood upright and held his weapon at ready. The girl dropped the unconscious canine boy to the floor and recalled her coils. They merged into a single, elongated whip.

"Who are you?!" Felix shouted. "What are you doing here!?"

"I followed you to see what you were up to! Why are you here?!"

"I followed him!" Felix gestured to the unconscious man down the hall between them. "He was trying to destroy this place. He freed that invader."

"You lie! You came here to destroy the repeater, too! Now you're gonna tell me why!"

"I'm not—"

Too late; the girl swung her elephant phallus. It stretched and elongated, but never thinned. Felix twisted the ring and encased the tip in a solid block of ice. The girl tried to lift it and break it against the wall, but by the time she realized what was happening Felix had created a glacier in the hallway. She struggled to free her weapon, but the ice was too thick. Felix climbed over the ice sheet and stood on the summit.

"Now you're gonna tell me where the others are, and what you're planning! Where is your leader?!"

She growled like a cat. "I'm not telling you anything!"

Felix was about to shout a witty comeback, but another explosion rocked the facility. The ice door bowed under the pressure. Hallways narrowed and buckled as the whole building shook. Felix fell from the top of the glacier and crashed to the floor.

The vibrations woke the man with the tommy gun canine. He stumbled to his feet and immediately ran for his weapon. He observed both Felix and the girl, turned around and made for the blast doors. He squeezed behind the knot and riddled the door with tiny canine bullets. They cut a large hole, and he sprinted through it, around the corner and out of sight.

Felix picked himself up. The girl struggled violently to free her weapon from the glacier.

"What's going on?!" shouted Felix. "Where are—"

The ice door shattered. Liquid sustenance gushed out the opening—it was a full meltdown.

Heat from the core melted the glacier just enough for her to free her weapon. Instead of going for Felix, she ran for the door. Felix followed her.

The girl slung her elephant weapon at the ceiling. It stuck to a support, pulled her up and swung her down the hallway.

Felix wished his weapon could do that. Then he remembered he had his own way! He aimed the weapon down and jumped on the flare and pogo'd, getting a few more steps ahead of the flow.

The girl swung from the rafters with her elephant penis. Felix pogo'd across the floor just feet in front of the river of fat. They traveled through doorways shot open by the man with the tommy gun canine.

With nothing to swing from anymore, the girl had to drop from the ceiling and leave on foot. She ran out the exit. Felix landed in front of the hole, bounced out at a low angle and sailed straight through without stopping.

As soon as Felix was out, the flow of liquid fat slowed enough for it to solidify and back up.

Felix landed atop a hill and looked back at the ruined repeater. The broadcast tower had collapsed and lay in pieces all around the facility. While he caught his breath, he realized the section he had just abandoned would probably be uninhabitable for as long as a thousand years. The half life for such highly concentrated grease was 100 years, and it would take at least ten half lives before it dissipated enough for human habitation.

The elephant girl and the tommy gun canine boy were nowhere to be seen. The Thor leveled up again, but Felix was too tired to notice.

# * Jellyfish Horse Modification *

"An elephant and a canine?" said the Sacred Horse.

"Yup. And they were hell bent on killing me."

"These people have been at the scene of every major incident. They must be responsible."

"I still haven't figured out their role," Felix said. "The one with the canine weapon looked like he was trying to kill that toaster in the supervisor."

"Seems likely an order had been given to destroy the repeater, and the signal to attack couldn't reach that far into the building. Or it's possible the managers in that room were interfering with the unit's ability to carry out its orders. Either way, the enemy had to send in ground forces. That could be the first part of their master plan, to destroy the sustenance broadcast system."

"Maybe. But she wanted to know what my plan was."

"She was the canine's bodyguard, sent to ensure the mission went smoothly. I believe that whole facility was a setup to draw you out. The enemy knows you are trying to stop it, but it wants to find out who you are working for and what you stand to gain."

"So the key to my survival is to make them believe I'm part of something bigger?"

"It may work. But the enemy will certainly try to lure you into another trap. You must be careful. Fortunately, the Thor just passed another level."

"Yeah, it grew a whole twelve inches."

The Thor Felix held was now orange colored and four feet tall. Twice its original length and girth, yet Felix could whip it around like a straw.

"I should warn you about this level, Felix. Now the Thor will inject anyone it touches with poison. Don't worry; it's smart enough not to inject you."

"A jellyfish mod! That'll come in handy next time I meet that girl. Let's see her try to grab me with that elephant again!"

The Sacred Horse smiled. "I knew you'd like this one."

"So now what?"

"Keep searching. You're bound to meet another agent of the enemy. Learn what you can, but reveal nothing about yourself. Let them believe there's more to you than meets the eye."

"Can do."

# * Why All Great Employees
# Drive a Minihearse *

Jarvis sleepwalked out the front door, locked it, and sleepwalked down the driveway to his Ford Minihearse. He opened the door, sat down in the driver's seat. Normally, vehicles performed retina scans to confirm the driver's identity, but the Minihearse was designed for the career man and measured Jarvis' REM pattern instead.

The engine started. The car backed out of the driveway. Jarvis' head rolled to the side as it turned the corner and drove down the road. The Minihearse was equipped with Smart Memory Ultimate Technology. This meant that it had memorized the route, knew the timing of the lights, the speed limits, even the routines of the other drivers he was most likely to encounter.

The car parked in Jarvis' normal spot. A sleeping Jarvis opened the door and hobbled to his feet. Briefcase in hand, he stumbled up the walk to the elevator, rode it up and sat down at his desk. Jarvis awoke there. He resumed working where he'd left off the previous day.

After his usual nineteen-hour workday, he collapsed from exhaustion.

Keeping this schedule for so long had conditioned his body to the routine. It knew when it was time to go, and automatically sleepwalked him to his car. The Minihearse drove him home. Jarvis sleepwalked out of the car, stumbled inside and collapsed in bed.

He slept there for exactly 45 minutes. Then his body swung his legs off the side of the bed, stood him up and walked him out the door. The Minihearse started, drove him the two hours to the office building. He sleepwalked out of the elevator and sat down at his desk. There, he woke up and began another nineteen-hour day.

His bosses were watching. Any activity that implied he was wasting company time would result in immediate termination, and there were a thousand other people with the same SM degree he had waiting to take his place. He had to be the perfect employee, and that meant working nineteen hours a day, every day, making the most efficient use of his time.

It was considered unprofessional to leave work fully awake. Obviously, the employee wasn't working hard enough if he wasn't asleep by the time he left. He couldn't sleep at the office; that would mean dozing on the job. Jarvis simply didn't have time to wait until he was home to sleep, so the proactive thing to do was multitask.

CBC had already eliminated the need to eat, so breaks were unnecessary. Jarvis hoped someday someone would eliminate the need for sleep so he wouldn't have to spend money on cars like the Minihearse. It was the reason the company paid him; so he could afford a Minihearse and be able to devote more time to the company.

Nineteen hours later, Jarvis keeled over from fatigue. He woke up again in the office. Jarvis was happy to have a career, and the work ethic to go with it. As far as he knew, home did not exist. The car did not exist. Every day he woke up at the office. Days blended together. Weeks. Months.

A crash interrupted Jarvis' sleep.

He woke up someplace not in his office. He didn't recognize it. He was in a bedroom. Was this his bedroom?

He heard thrashing in the living room. Screaming and shouting and cursing and what sounded like ice shards hitting the walls. Jarvis swung out of bed and stormed into the living room.

His front door was wide open. It looked like the lock had been stretched. A man in red was in his house, chasing a toaster around the room, aiming a gigantic piece of horse anatomy at it. Ice shards shot from the tip. The toaster dodged the man's attacks.

Idly, Jarvis wondered why he had a toaster in the first place. His was a modern house; it didn't even have a kitchen. Where had that toaster come from? And why was he upset that this man was trying to kill it?

The toaster dive-bombed the man in red. With the agility of a superhero, the man rolled out of the way, landed nobly on one knee, horse penis tucked under his arm like a shotgun. He twisted the ring and fired more ice shards. The toaster did a loop around the spray and dove at the man again.

No time to roll this time; the man lunged forward, slid on Jarvis' carpet and stopped in the middle of the floor. The toaster sailed up the wall, banked left and hovered in place. The man righted himself, took aim and iced again.

Jarvis leaned on the doorframe, stood up straight and said, "What are you doing in my house?" Jarvis said this confidently, but didn't feel like he had a right to be angry. Mostly because he wasn't certain this was his house.

His words drew the attention of both toaster and the man in red. The man faced him. The flow of ice stopped. The toaster also glared at Jarvis. It beeped, and swept straight for the man with the career.

"NOO!" Jarvis screamed as the toaster slammed into his gut.

Thankfully, his body was very well conditioned. It still went to work the following day, but now Jarvis didn't need to sleep. He worked 24/7. His car sat in the parking lot, unused. His body slowly decomposed, but the routine had become so engrained in his body that his bones had memorized it. Even as flesh rotted, he was still able to work, and he didn't need breaks, didn't need to go home, didn't demand to be paid, didn't complain or object to anything.

This excited the managers greatly. Finally, they had found their ideal employee and promoted him to senior management, and he lived happily ever after.

# * Crossing Swords *

Felix sat down on the bench in the courtyard between the skyscrapers. The sky was cloudy and it hid the moon. Felix was awash in majestic, artificial light. He relaxed and absorbed sustenance.

He cried.

For the first time, one of the toasters had claimed a victim. The incident at the CBC repeater was not directly his fault. He hadn't released that toaster; he hadn't allowed the thing to reach the core and destroy the place. But that man tonight... Felix was responsible for his death.

In the last week, he had destroyed a hundred more toasters, but his search for another person wielding a weapon such as his had come up empty. He was beginning to doubt this whole epic quest thing was such a good idea. There were so many toasters spread out over such long distances.

Perhaps the rules of epic quests were written long ago, when people lived much farther apart and there was no communication between them. Threats to the human species weren't as widespread back then as they are today. Felix sensed there had to be a more modern way of going about this.

He began to feel very sleepy. Using the Thor as a pillow, he rested on the bench. Quickly, he drifted off to sleep. Felix did not dream, but he did sleep through all of the next day and into the following night.

Something woke him up. He opened his eyes slowly. Someone was standing over him. The figure's face was backlit against the artificial skyscraper light.

As Felix registered what was happening, he woke up and started to reach for his weapon, but the figure held him down. Against his neck, Felix felt a weapon shaped like some animal's anatomy, but razor sharp.

"Don't move," said a male voice.

Felix did not.

"Who are you?" it continued.

Felix swallowed. His mind spun. He'd gotten out of tight scrapes before; he just needed time to think.

"My name is Felix."

"Who do you work for?"

"I work for no one."

"You lie."

"Why would I do that?"

"You tell me."

"Well, I might lie to conceal my true intentions."

"Naturally."

"And I might lie to make myself sound more important than I really am."

"I'd believe that."

"I might also lie to hide the fact that I'm telling the truth."

"Come again?"

"Since I'm not lying, I might tell a lie to satisfy you so we can move on."

"Or to conceal your plan."

"Who said I have a plan?"

"Everyone has a plan."

"Not everyone."

"Sure they do."

"No, they don't."

"Of course they do."

"Do I look like I have a plan?"

"Yes."

"What makes you say that?"

"Because of the weapon you carry."

"Well you carry a weapon. What's your plan?"

"Who said I had a plan?"

"You did."

"What if I lied?"

"Are you saying you're more important than you are?"

"No, I have a plan."

"What is it?"

"To find out what your plan is."

"Why me?"

"Because you carry a weapon like mine."

"What weapon is yours?"

"I wield the Aslan, a lion, level twenty-one."

"Is that so? I wield the Thor, a horse, level thirty-seven."

"Yours levels up, too? Mine can cut through anything and shoots lightning."

"Mine shoots ice and has a jellyfish mod."

"Yours has poison?"

"Yeah. How big is yours?"

"About four feet."

Felix grinned. "Hah! Mine's up to five!"

"What? No way!"

"I'll prove it."

"Let's see!"

The man let Felix up, and he lifted his Thor. The man held his Aslan beside it. No contest. The Thor won.

"Damn, you're huge!" said the man. "How do you even use something that big?!"

"I've had lots of practice over the last three months."

"That's the same time I got mine! How did yours get so big so fast?"

"Maybe I'm just better."

"Bullshit! Mine cuts through anything. What's yours do?"

"It magnifies my swinging power by about fifty times, I figure. One of the earliest levels allowed me to use it like a pogo stick."

"Pffft. Thor indeed; it's about as graceful as a Neanderthal's club. My weapon is like a fine, Japanese sword."

"Really? Well let's see how well you handle it."

"You're on!"

They walked to the middle of the park and stood at weapon's length apart. For a moment, they stared at each other. Felix remained resolute. His prowess with his weapon had been questioned; he was determined not to be bested by someone smaller.

The man made the first move. He swung his weapon into the Thor. The impact surprised Felix. It was much stronger than he had expected, and it pushed his Thor to the ground. The Aslan merely held it in place.

The man was a bit stunned. "It didn't cut through!" he shouted.

Felix arced his weapon, repelling the Aslan and throwing the man back a few steps. Swirling the Thor over his head, Felix slammed it down where the man stood. The man dove out of the way, rolled and crouched on the grass.

Felix swung the Thor laterally, trying to swipe the man from the side. His opponent charged, Aslan held like a lance. Felix deflected it with the Thor. The man jumped into the deflection, swinging the Aslan to behead Felix with an inward stroke. Felix ducked and raised the Thor between himself and the Aslan. The lion weapon connected with the horse and stopped. Felix shoved it away and rolled out of striking distance. The man charged again.

Felix and his opponent sparred ferociously. They attacked, dodged, parried, thrust, gave, took, pitched, caught, leaped and pranced. Neither engaged their projectile mods. For some reason,

Felix felt that would be a breach of some sort of etiquette.

The man took aim for Felix's face. Instead, the Aslan connected with the Thor's preputial ring and stuck there. It was as good as the hilt of a sword, so Felix raised the Thor, throwing off the Aslan. The man leaped backwards and dodged Felix's blow with only an inch to spare.

Felix halted in cat stance. The man with the Aslan had just finished a triple toeloop and landed gracefully on the grass with one foot. They stood. Motionless. Studying one another. Neither decided to make the next move. Instead, they simply bowed.

"You wield your Thor quite well, Felix."

"What is your name?"

"Norman."

"You are skilled with your Aslan, Norman."

"Thank you. I must take my leave of you, Felix. Perhaps we will meet again."

"I hope I share in equal measure. Farewell."

They turned around and dashed off into the night

Felix dashed for a solid mile before he realized he didn't have a place to dash off to. He stopped. He looked around. Pedestrians walked to and fro. Cars honked horns. Stoplights clicked red, green and yellow.

"Crap!"

Felix smacked himself upside the head with the Thor. He fell head over heels and landed on his back, unconscious.

# * Heroes and Sex Toys *

"What do you mean you forgot to interrogate him!?" shouted the Sacred Horse.

"I…uh… Well, we pulled our weapons out. He was a bit jealous of my size, so he started comparing mods… That led to a little contest…"

"Contest? You had the chance to find out what's going on, and you wasted it on a ridiculous contest?! What were you thinking??!!"

"Well, I just woke up…and I'd never seen one even close to my size before, and I was curious. I know I messed up, but I'm sure I'll have another chance."

"And how many more lives will be lost because of your mistake?! We have no idea when the final attack will come, and you blew your one opportunity crossing swords with some stranger!"

"I'm sorry, but I've been meaning to ask you about the method of this quest."

"What method?"

"The method of taking out toasters one at a time. I mean, yes, the Thor is the greatest weapon ever, but don't you think this whole thing is a little… Uh… Inefficient?"

"Can you think of a better way to do it?!"

"Well, yes, actually… I could use the Thor to get on TV or something and tell people the danger that may be lurking in their stomachs, or in their homes. I could get them to bring their toasters to me instead of—"

"That would alert the enemy to our intentions! It would gather all the toasters together in one area, which for all we know is exactly what the enemy wants us to do!"

"Or… Maybe the enemy wants us to keep doing it this way to buy him more time to prepare for the final strike."

The Sacred Horse growled. Felix didn't know horses could growl, but guessed if one had a Sacred Sheath, one could do anything one pleased.

"Epic quests don't involve the internet or TV! They involve sex toys and manly, hard-bodied, larger-than-life heroes defying physics, logic and insurmountable odds, spitting out quotable, highly marketable catchphrases all the while! Humanity has been saved this way for thousands of years! It DOESN'T! NEED! TO CHANGE!"

If he were still working at the store, Felix would've bent over and cowered when a manager yelled at him like that. But he had grown up in the last three months. He stood his ground. He used his customer-service-enhanced speech skills and responded evenly.

"The world didn't have ten billion people living in it thousands of years ago. Communication between villages didn't exist, and the only way anyone heard of these heroes was through bards strumming a harp. You call that a heroic way to be remembered?"

The Horse breathed hard. Fast.

"Times have changed," Felix said. "Maybe it's time to rethink how we're going about this."

Felix could see he had reached the Sacred Horse. He was considering it. Gradually, he calmed down.

"This has been rather tedious hasn't it?" the Horse said, finally.

"Yeah. Something a consultant wouldn't notice, I'll bet," Felix said with a smirk.

The Horse returned the smirk. "I agree. I'd like to find a better way, but we can't alert the enemy. For all we know, as soon as we go public, that's when the toasters will detonate. Goodbye city. Goodbye humanity."

"I understand. But there's gotta be a better way."

"Perhaps there is. If you think of one, let me know. If I think of one, I'll let you know. In the meantime, get your quest back on track. Remain stealthy. It's the safest way to fight this. And next time don't miss your chance to get more information."

"All right. And I won't. I just got carried away with the power of my weapon, that's all. Happens to even the most hard-bodied of heroes, doesn't it?"

The Sacred Horse smiled. It was good to see a smile on his face again. "You have no idea. Keep working on your catchphrases. They're not very marketable yet."

"Yeah, all my catchphrases are lame."

The Horse winked. "Wait 'til you're all the way leveled up; you'll get there."

"Oh, cool!"

"And have you been practicing your preachy speeches? I haven't heard any preachiness from you yet."

"Oh...uh, well, no, not really."

"You don't want to be caught in a speech situation and deliver a dud when you could've saved the world."

"I think I've got it. I'm customer service, after all."

The Horse nodded. "No debating that. Good luck, warrior."

# * The Perfect Cop *

The unemployment line wrapped around the building twice. Hundreds were in it, waiting for a chance to browse the current list of available jobs and try their luck. Inevitably, the graduates left in defeat and walked out onto the streets to sleep and hope for a better tomorrow.

Some were lucky enough to own cardboard boxes. The ones who weren't resourceful enough to obtain a box coveted their neighbor's. Box theft had long ago been elevated to grand larceny status, and police patrolled the city tirelessly, waiting for a chance to catch a box thief.

One of these police officers, Mike, walked calmly up and down the line of graduates. He scrutinized them all. He empathized with them; he used to be in one of these lines. He had a masters degree in Avian SM, and, after living under a cardboard box for twelve years, trying to use his qualification and running from town to town to stay one step ahead of the debt collectors (who, for some reason, claimed he owed thousands of dollars to a company called CBC), he finally landed a job.

He was one of the lucky ones to survive in his job for longer than a week. He figured by now he must have convinced his superiors that he was one of the rare, perfect police officers. Never questioned orders, worked round the clock and didn't ask for time off, or to be paid. If he received a reward for his work, he wouldn't turn it down, but he didn't work for money. He worked because he was grateful to be an employed and productive member of society. He was exactly what employers looked for. At least until a type of robot was invented that could do this job.

Some commotion was coming from the back of the line. Mike walked toward the sound. There, in the distance, was a man out of line, walking up to every ninth graduate and stabbing him or her in the stomach with some sort of sex toy.

Mike mentally flipped through his Rolodex of law. He couldn't think of a law this man was breaking (there were just college graduates after all—like heads of the hydra) but still, something about it seemed wrong.

He walked up to the man just as he stabbed a well-nourished girl. The girl puffed. Black smoke spewed from her mouth, ears and vagina. She regained her composure and continued standing in line. The man with the toy began running, but Mike held up a hand.

"Excuse me, sir. What are you doing?"

"I'm saving the world!"

"I beg your pardon?"

"Yeah, I've never seen so many of these things in one place! I got lucky today!"

"You don't say?"

"Yeah… In fact…" The man aimed the dildo at the officer's stomach. The horse penis vibrated like a dousing rod. Then it thrust Mike through the gut.

An explosion roared in Mike's ears. He coughed smoke. Smoke spewed out the back of his pants.

"And another one!" exclaimed the man. "I'm on a roll today!"

Mike swayed.

"Don't worry; I turned off the acid. All these people are perfectly fine. They'll be better than ever now they're toaster-free!"

"I didn't know I had a toaster," Mike coughed.

"Hardly anyone seems to be aware of it. I'da thought it was obvious, but people are so surprised when I liberate them. Do you feel liberated?"

Mike thought about that. He did feel lighter, and the smoke had cleansed his insides of the heavy feeling that had held his spirit down for years. So, "Yes. I think I do."

"Then my job here is done! Away! Away I go, like an arrow shot from a bow!"

The man skipped past Mike, further on down the line.

Mike wobbled for a minute before finding equilibrium.

"Carry on," he said.

He walked up the line. His footsteps felt lighter, and he bounced. The bounce in his step turned into a skip. It was not something a professional police officer would do, and he was sure his bosses would see it and use it as an excuse to fire him and hire someone else from this line who could be molded and terrified into the perfect officer, but Mike didn't care. It felt strangely good to be free of the extra weight.

# * What a Twist *

Felix knelt on the rooftop of a high building. He looked out over the beautiful cityscape. The glass façades that reflected starlight and glittered. The clogged traffic in the streets far below. The office skyscrapers, still alive with light and figures moving within. Inside, Felix knew, terrified employees worked 'round the clock. They were the real patriots. The true heroes of this great nation.

He gazed out over the west side of the city. A twenty square block swath of it was dark. Too sustenance-concentrated to support life. Normally the moon would be out, but the thick grease that hovered over this region blotted out the sky. Smoke from burning cars contributed to the darkness as well.

Birds that flew into this zone instantly swelled from two ounces of feathers and bone to fifty pounds of solid fat, died and careened to the ground. Their beaks sometimes penetrated automobile gas tanks. Felix watched one of these explosions now.

And another.

And another.

A beautiful city. Felix rocked back and sat down, admiring the view, six-foot weapon (now colored lava red from its last level) draped across his lap. He watched the unmoving traffic. He watched the shadows of workers in the buildings dash around. He watched swollen birds fall out of the sky and slam into gas tanks.

A toaster flapped by. Felix did a double-take. He got to his feet, raised his Thor and was about to throw it like a spear when, in the distance, he glimpsed another toaster rise into the air.

Felix lowered his weapon, and eight more flapped silently into view. A minute later, he heard the collective grunts of a thousand people as their toasters crawled out the slit in their guts. A thousand toasters ascended majestically to the tops of the skyscrapers. Windows shattered as they flew out of high-rise buildings and houses.

Felix stood there, Thor draped across his shoulders, staring. His first instinct was to launch some ice at one of the toasters and try to cause a series of chain reaction explosions, but he wondered about the debris storm that would cause. Right now, the sight was so awe inspiring he couldn't look away. The hazed moon backlit the massive flock of toasters hovering over the cityscape.

Like birds that know instinctually which direction to fly and when to do it, the toasters flapped gracefully towards the east side of the city. People in office buildings paused to look. The executives saw them, fired them, picked up an equal number of people from the unemployment lines and set them to work in their place.

Felix observed the flow. They were slowly heading to the bad part of town. He leapt from the building, fell all 200 stories and landed squarely on the Thor's tip. Felix didn't have to pogo amongst traffic anymore, or weave through buildings. His last upgrade increased his pogo stick ability, and he was able to scale entire skyscrapers with minimal effort.

He propelled himself up the glass face of one 400-story office building. Then another. And another. He traveled with the flock without interfering with it. The toasters didn't seem to notice. They never looked at him, never wavered from their collective purpose.

On the east side of town, the flock began to bend downwards. Felix landed on a rooftop and watched. The toasters were funneling down, down, down, and into an abandoned warehouse's open door.

Felix pogo'd from the building, landed softly on the sidewalk and ran the rest of the way. Toasters flapped gently overhead, spreading out across the warehouse.

Standing in the warehouse's center, looking up in awe at the flock above him, was a teenager holding a small weapon. Felix had never seen a dragon before, but he knew a dragon's penis when he saw it.

Felix didn't give him time to prepare; he raised the Thor, twisted the ring and launched a spray of glacial ice. The teenager heard the sound and barreled out of the way. A small glacier formed where he'd been standing.

The teenager rolled to a stop on one knee. His Ridgeback, which at first was merely nine inches long, instantly swelled to five feet. He squeezed the base.

Felix felt a force wrap around him. The teenager raised the Ridgeback high, and Felix flew up with it to the ceiling. He was now in the cloud of toasters, but instead of colliding with him and exploding, they avoided him. The teenager swept him further into the crowd, but the toasters were careful not to touch him.

Cursing, the teenager lowered his grip on the Ridgeback. Felix dropped from the air, straight towards the concrete floor. Felix had just enough time to align the Thor at the right angle. When he hit the ground, the pogo stick mod sent him hurtling back into the toaster cloud. Felix's arms flailed wildly, and, in his confusion, he grabbed a couple toasters.

He expected to fall straight down, taking the appliances with him. Instead, the toasters carried him as they continued flying through the warehouse. Cloaked in the flock, Felix held on. When he guessed he was in the right place, Felix dropped down.

He landed softly on the concrete behind the teenager, still looking up at the flock for Felix. Felix dashed up to him, raised his weapon and swung.

At the last second, the teenager heard this and raised his own weapon. He blocked, but the force of the Thor still carried through and knocked the teenager across the floor and into a wall.

The flock of toasters overhead was starting to thin out.

The teenager got to his feet. Felix sent out more glacier shards. The teenager caught them with his sex toy, turned them around and sent them back to Felix. Felix wound up, swung, and smacked the shards back to the teenager, who caught them telekinetically and sent them back to Felix, who sent them back to the teenager, who sent them back to Felix.

Finally, the teenager shook his head and simply dove out of the way. The shards froze the wall behind him. He swung his Ridgeback, squeezed the shaft. It puffed up, and out popped a tiny dragon.

Felix stood and stared. It was cute. More like a stuffed animal than a monster. Then the tiny dragon grew. And grew. And GREW. And GREW!!! It went from hatchling to a hulking, muscular twenty-foot long monster in four seconds. It inhaled and spat a fireball at Felix.

He swung the Thor and hit the fireball back to the dragon. It was not expecting this, and just stood there while the fireball screamed towards it. Direct hit between the eyes. The dragon dissolved into the air, exposing the teenager who had been hiding behind it. He was just as surprised as the dragon had been.

"Is that all your weapon can do?" Felix shouted.

The teenager cursed again, aimed his telekinetic mod at Felix, but Felix had already begun spraying ice. Quickly, the teenager jumped out of the way before it could cover his feet. Felix was about to launch more ice at him, but the teenager hesitated and suddenly focused his attention behind Felix. Felix took the chance and glanced over his shoulder.

Standing in the open bay doors was a man holding a kangaroo phallus. His weapon was bigger now than when Felix first saw it.

He took aim, squeezed the shaft—

—Felix knew what was coming and dove out of the way—

—and fired a laser from the tip—

—just as fireballs flew down from the ceiling. Felix looked up at the girl in the air. Her dolphin anatomy had grown, but it still formed a protective shield around her. Felix was getting good at this; he swung his Thor and returned the girl's fire. She strafed out of the way. A fireball hit the concrete floor, where it disturbed a guy holding an elongated rabbit penis who was trying to launch a missile at the man with the tommy gun canine.

The warehouse was suddenly swarming with people, all carrying animal weapons. The Ridgeback dodged laser fire from the kangaroo. The canine came under attack from someone with a very upgraded eagle's anatomy. Members whacked and collided; attackers parried and dodged. Fire, electricity and beams of charged tachyon particles flew everywhere.

Immediately, Felix was swept up in the fray. He engaged a woman with an upgraded lizard's tool for a while, trying to make his way to the teenager with the Ridgeback.

The lizard weapon gave the woman the power of multiplicity, and Felix wasted so much time attacking her phantom clones he never landed a blow on the real person. He didn't have to; she became occupied defending herself from the boy wielding the panda.

Felix seized the opportunity and made for the Ridgeback. He knew how to get him isolated. He swung the Thor above his head, around and around. The Thor collected the air and spun a cyclone around them. While the teenager was trying to get a grip on what was happening, Felix jumped him and pinned him to the ground. The tornado would only last a minute without the Thor stirring the winds, so he had to do this quickly.

Felix held the tip of the Thor to the teenager's chest. The teenager got the point and remained spread-eagle, useless Ridgeback out to the side.

"Call off your forces!" Felix shouted over the wind. "You can't win now."

"*My* forces?!" said the teenager. "Call off yours! You'll never succeed in destroying humanity!"

"I'm not trying to destroy humanity! I'm here to protect it!"

"So am I!"

"Liar!" shouted Felix. "You've been calling the shots from the beginning, planting toasters all over the city, maybe the world! I want to know why!"

The teenager regarded Felix for a breath. "So do I!"

The look in the teenager's eyes was so sincere, so bewildered, that all the fight Felix had left him. The tornado died. The others continued fighting. Fire and tachyons and wind and vore attacks filled the warehouse, as well as the sound of colliding sex toys.

Felix stepped back. "What's your name?"

"Joey." He stood up, Ridgeback aimed at the ground.

"I'm Felix. You're…not the mastermind behind this whole thing?"

"No. You're not either?"

"I thought you were. I met an insider who told me a person carrying a Ridgeback was the one calling the shots."

"Who told you that?"

"Someone named Pat."

"Pat? Pat's Novelty Toaster Corporation?"

"Yeah, him. You know him?"

"He told me a kid with a horse weapon was behind this!"

Just then, Felix's back was on fire. He rolled to put the fire out. When he hopped to his feet, he found himself staring at the tip of the dolphin's fiery penis. His gaze continued upwards to the girl hovering in the air. Her shield was weaker now; she must have taken a beating. She held Felix at dolphinpoint.

"You! Call off your henchmen! Then we can discuss what that factory was cranking out!"

"I was investigating it. What were you doing there?"

"I was led there, and I saw you patrolling it!"

"I wasn't patrolling. I thought you were running the place and destroyed it to keep me from learning more about it."

"I destroyed it because I thought it was your hub."

Some of the others had overheard them and paused fighting their opponents to listen.

"You're not in charge, either?" Felix said.

"Why would you think I was!?" said the girl. "I was called to save the human race from an alien threat! Instead, I find a factory!"

"I was called to save the world, too," Felix said.

The girl lowered the dolphin. Her shield lowered as well. The sounds of fighting died gradually. Felix looked around. He found the kangaroo boy and pointed at him.

"Hey, you! Who are you? I saw you on the rooftop. What were you doing there?"

Joey grabbed the man by telekinesis and carried him to interview distance of Felix.

"I'm, uh, Peter. I saw you attack that guy in the crowd. I thought you were implanting a toaster. Pat told me a girl with an elephant weapon was the mastermind behind this."

The girl with the elephant weapon and the boy with the canine weapon both stepped forward.

"Well, I ain't in charge," said the girl. "What the hell's going on here? What happened at that repeater station?"

"I'm Felix. I went there to take out two threats," he said. "Then you showed up." Felix pointed at the canine boy. "I followed you to see what you were up to."

"Gary," said the canine boy. "I went there to destroy that toaster, too. It got away. Someone in the toaster factory told me a kid with a rabbit dick was in charge."

"I'm Jill," said the elephant girl. "I followed Felix on the orders of the Sacred Elephant."

"Sacred Elephant?" Felix said. "Do you know the Sacred Horse?"

"Never heard of him."

The others in the warehouse asked if anyone knew the Sacred Dolphin, Hyena, Wolf, Dragon, Eagle, and so on.

As one, they called out to their Sacred Animals. Windows to heaven opened, and the Sacred Animals saw each other. All were taken aback. They never knew there were other Sacred Animals. They mingled through their windows. All the wielders mingled, too.

Felix was curious how Joey got his Ridgeback.

"I have a DSM degree," Joey said with pride.

"Really? Where are the dragons?"

"They're easy to find. You just have to believe."

"Oh. Sure... Wait, you have an SM? At your age?"

"Yeah, I'm seventeen. I took a lot of advanced courses in high school. Guidance counselors saw me drawing dragons and encouraged me to pursue my dream, so I got a head start."

All at once, everyone revealed they all had non-human SM degrees. Lapine, elephant, dolphin, feline... Felix was the only Equine in the bunch. Someone had started making tea, and everyone sat down, drank and compared notes.

Felix had the biggest weapon. Longest, thickest, most mods, most power. Out of all seventeen people, he was the most leveled up. They joked this must make him the leader.

"Maybe. But leader of what?"

They debated this over tea. Afterwards, the Sacred Animals addressed the group. They had never seen other Sacred Animals before, let alone ones that loved humanity enough to give up their penises, too. Like Felix speculated, thousands of years ago the distance between villages was much greater, and word took longer to travel

73

from town to town, nation to nation. The same limits applied to the animals as well.

"Um…" said the girl with the lizard weapon. "I'm glad to know who we're working for, but who are we fighting?"

The warehouse was silent.

"And where did the toasters go?" Joey said.

# * A Long Exposition Monologue
# in the Middle of the Action*

The air was still pregnant with the question.

Gears cranked beneath the group. The concrete floor folded rapidly and sent all seventeen perverts tumbling down to what appeared to be a modest laboratory. A sphere of energy surrounded them in mid-air, holding them in place. An old man stared at them, hands behind his back.

"Pat?!" said Felix.

The man scowled. "Hello, everyone."

"That's him!" said a bunch of people at once.

"He told me the canine was behind all of this!" said the boy with the meerkat weapon.

"You said the lion was—"

"—the sheep was behind—"

"—eagle was masterminding—!"

And so on...

Pat paced in front of the sphere, waiting for everyone to stop talking.

"Yes, I knew you would follow the toasters and meet up. To answer your question, I sent them back to their stations. You didn't notice, did you, that the toasters flew straight through the warehouse? Too busy fighting each other, just as I hoped—but you were supposed to destroy each other! You weren't supposed to TALK OVER TEA!"

The man stopped and looked across the group.

"I created the toasters because I already owned a toaster factory, and they were easy to convert to a delivery system for the explosives that would blend in easily no matter where it was. I've been waiting for the right moment to strike for years."

"But why?" said Joey.

"Have any of you noticed the element common to all my toaster victims?"

The wielders shook their heads collectively.

"They have degrees! Specifically, degrees in some form of animal SM. Did you know there was a time when you didn't need a degree to be a pervert? You did it all by yourself, in secret, because you didn't do it to make money, you did it for the personal satisfaction, and that's how you got good at it! I was managing stress in felines for the San Diego Zoo before all of you were even born! I had it made! I was respected in my field; I was rich; I had love; I received hazardous duty pay; I lacked nothing!

"Then colleges started offering courses in animal stress management. My bosses told me I wasn't qualified for the job I'd been doing for twenty years. They hired a college rookie to replace me. Because the labor market was so saturated, they didn't have to pay him. They convinced him—everyone!—that it was acceptable to work for the privilege of being employed!

"I waited in unemployment lines for years, hoping for a job. I got several, only to be kicked out the next day and replaced by someone else! Nobody would look at me because I had no degree, and yet I knew some of those so-called SM professors. I knew more than they did! I knew more than all you kids put together, and I was treated like an ignorant old man!

"I had to take a job manufacturing toasters! I hated it, but it was a job, and I was grateful for it like everyone should be. I even started up my own toaster company. Two years later the CBC came. Made food obsolete. Made me obsolete *again*! My company became a novelty factory and did a fraction of the business it used to!

"I plotted my revenge! I researched ways to turn my novelties into weapons. I created software that allowed toasters to seek out everyone with SM degrees and implant themselves in their bodies. All the pieces were in place! I was almost ready to deliver my swift and final blow to the SM holders—simultaneous detonation! It would leave me the only person in the world qualified to manage animal stress! ME! They couldn't dismiss me, or make me work for nothing but the privilege of having a job! I'd get the life I deserved back! The life you kids stole from me!

"But then the Sacred Weapons started showing up. Seems my grand scheme was large enough to attract the attention of ancient prophesy. You started destroying my toasters, interfering with my perfect plans! I captured one of you, found out everything he knew. I figured there had to be more than one, and I was right. You didn't know that others had been sent on the same quest. I fed you false information, tried to get you to turn on each other, and it almost worked! I was going to draw you back to the factory, but SOMEONE destroyed it! Had to make a backup plan, which was to contain you here."

Pat paused. Felix felt free to stick in a word.

"Why toasters? Why not just implant people with explosives?"

"To make people believe the world was victim of some sort of alien attack, thereby focusing suspicion away from me."

"Toasters?"

"They fly; they're sinister; they have to be alien!"

Felix blinked. "Toasters?"

"It worked, didn't it? Had the Sacred Animals fooled."

The wielders murmured.

"I expect you'll keep us here so we can witness your great victory," Felix said.

"Hell with that. I'm not stupid like all the other supervillains with vendettas against the society that rejected them. I'm just gonna kill you."

Pat turned around and walked to the control panel. He pressed a button. The forcefield began to close in. The wielders huddled together and whimpered.

But someone raised his weapon. It was in the shape of giraffe.

"Quick! Does anyone have gravitons?"

"I do!" shouted the man with an eagle weapon.

"Tachyons!?"

"Me!" said a man holding a hyena.

"My giraffe is a pre-modified deflector dish! Aim your weapons at mine!"

The two volunteers did this, and the hyena emitted tachyons while the eagle emitted gravitons. They bounced off the deflector dildo, which created a quantumly entangled electromagnetic dispersion field that disrupted the energy sphere. It fizzled out harmlessly just before it closed around everyone's head. Felix smiled. He jumped from the platform and dashed towards Pat, a whole army of Stress Management Specialists behind him.

Pat spun around, braced himself on the desk. "No! Impossible!" He slammed his fists on another button. A door in the wall slid open; a laser emerged. Radioactive symbols were painted on it.

"STOP!" cried Pat.

Felix and the rest of the army halted.

"Your weapons can shield you from radiation," shouted the old man, "but I'll bet there's an upper limit! You will not ruin my plan!"

"You and your blasphemous ideals will never defeat our glorious capitalist system!" Felix shouted.

"Glorious! You speak of glory and prosperity, but who prospers!? Certainly not me! Not you! The ones who prosper are those who have the power to hire you for no pay, and nobody can oppose them because of mile-long unemployment lines around every building in the city!"

"Those lines are the backbone of this great nation!" Felix preached. "We are now the global leader in industry and commerce! Our nation needs employment saturation to remain competitive in the world market! You cannot stand in the way of the ideal of corporate rule and cheap, disposable labor!"

Felix felt very proud of himself for making that speech. He felt it had an 86% chance of reaching someone and changing his worldview. Pat swayed in the face of such profound truth. Felix felt himself gain 50 XP for speech success.

"Your preachy monologues are very good. I can tell I'm no match for you, so I shall have to make myself an even bigger supervillain! You see this ray? It's actually a leftover cooling rod from a power plant. I used it to research the propulsion system for my army of toasters! I may not be a pervert with a heart pure enough to wield a sacred weapon, but I will blast myself with radiation and give myself super powers. Then nothing will stop me from pressing the button and detonating my army when the time is right!"

Pat laughed manically, slammed a button and jumped in front of the laser barrel. The laser charged up. Everyone but the man with the cheetah weapon dove out of the way, their weapons telling them this was going to be too much.

An amber light atop the laser rotated. Pat stood on the platform and absorbed the radiation, still laughing. Ten seconds later, the laser powered down. Pat turned and faced the army cowering against the walls.

"Well?" Jill, the elephant girl, said.

"I… Don't understand…" Pat said. "Radiation always gives people super powers. I figured I'd start growing by now. Give me another minute; let's see what happens."

They waited. The cheetah still stood in the middle of the room, holding his weapon with confidence, apparently unaffected. The other wielders murmured amongst themselves.

Minutes passed. Pat screamed. He vomited blood and diarrhea. His hair didn't merely fall out, but exploded from his epidermis. His skin turned black, bubbled up and separated from his muscles and bones.

Pat ran out of screams; his mouth hung open soundlessly. His bones withered into toothpicks and snapped all at once. Tumors sprouted like baseballs on what was left of his skin. Cancerous cysts ballooned in his bones, thickening them out again.

He collapsed to the floor, motionless.

The army ventured slowly from the relative safety of the walls and gawked at the mess on the floor. Someone coughed. After staring at Pat's lifeless body for nearly a minute, someone spoke.

"Should we keep waiting?"

"No, I think we're done," Felix said. He glanced at Pat again. "Yeah, we're done." He shuddered and walked to the control panel.

Felix looked at the big red button, no doubt the one that would order the entire fleet of toasters to detonate. A matrix of smaller buttons surrounded it.

"Anyone have an idea which button might bring back the fleet?" Felix called over his shoulder.

"Could be any one of them," said a girl with a hyena weapon.

"Hey!" said a voice from the army. "Mine is a hacking tool!"

"We can all pick locks," somebody else said.

"No, mine hacks electronics!"

"Good," said Felix, waving the kid towards him. "See if you can interface with this stuff. We need to recall all the toasters…then we can figure out what to do with them."

The boy made his way through the crowd. He carried a piece of whale's anatomy, colored sunshine yellow. The others stepped aside as he passed, and he stood at the consol. He placed his member on it and pressed a hand against the other side.

"It's wireless! It'll be easy to interface."

"Excellent. Get to work." Felix patted him on the back and walked up to the laser.

"We should get rid of this thing. Anyone have something that can?"

"My cheetah neutralizes radiation, but only around me."

"All right. Anyone else?"

"Uh, I have a meerkat," a boy said. "It's a transmogrifier with vore attack mod. It can eat anything smaller than it, and changes small objects into flowers. That's how I've been dealing with the toasters on my epic quest."

"Hmmmm…possible. Anyone have anything else?"

The room was silent.

"Flowers it is. Step up. Can you change this whole laser?"

"Uh…no. I could do the cooling rod, but not the whole thing."

"Then you, cheetah. Neutralize the radiation while we take this laser apart. Norman? Where are you?"

Three people stepped out of the crowd. The boy with the cheetah activated his radiation neutrality field. Norman stayed within the field and began cutting apart the laser's housing. The transmogrifier meerkat stood by.

There were still a lot of people just milling around. Felix shouted to them.

"The rest of us, let's begin disassembling this place. Look out for anything useful, dangerous or unusual."

The crowd separated and began searching the laboratory, taking desks apart, opening file cabinets and rifling through Pat's sock drawer. Felix felt proud of himself. So this is what it felt like to be a manager. He could get accustomed to using employees as disposable extensions of himself.

Then, moaning. Felix looked down. The cancerous lump of flesh and bone moved. Felix's eyes widened. Pat rose majestically. Felix couldn't see how he was doing it; his muscles were tattered pieces of goo hanging off his bones, just like his decayed skin.

Pat straightened up.

"I knew radiation wouldn't fail me!" he roared. Everyone in the laboratory turned and faced him. "It has transformed my body and my mind! My chaotic cell structure gives me unlimited strength and the ability to fly!"

"Whaaat?!" Felix said. "How the hell do you know that?!"

"I have become radiation! The nucleus is now part of me, and I sense it in its infinite complexity! I am one with it! I understand everything now!"

"That doesn't make sense!"

"Hey, I'm a pervert, not a scientist! And now I have the power to destroy all of you and complete my plan!"

"But you'll never be an SMS now!" shouted Felix.

"I don't have to be anymore! I have evolved beyond the need to manage stress in animals! Now I can focus on the real enemy! The bigger picture! I shall wipe out all the universities and graduates in the world! I shall restore our nation to its former glory, by reinstating labor unions, decreasing labor supply and putting power back in the hands of the people!"

The wielders stood as one. They stared as one. They shouted as one, "NOOOOOOOO!"

"So it's come down to this," said Pat. "Pure capitalism verses limited capitalism, chaos verses order, good verses evil, science verses dogma! A battle not merely taking place in the superficial realm, but in the depths of allegorical ideals! Perfect! This is all legit!"

With a laugh, Pat launched himself into the air. He hovered above the crowd, just below the concrete ceiling of the warehouse.

The elephant girl whipped her weapon at Pat. Its long coil

stretched up to him and wrapped around his ankle. The cancer was so strong it spread to the weapon. Cysts and balls of random cells started growing on it. The elephant panicked and released him. After severing the damaged part, it recoiled back to the girl.

Pat held up his hands. Cancerous cysts formed on his palms. He tossed the cysts. Some exploded on the floor, covering those nearby in cancerous matter. Wielders fell to the ground screaming as the cells worked their way into their bodies and multiplied uncontrollably. The matter that didn't touch flesh grew like vines, spreading along the floors and walls.

Felix leaped into the crowd. After making sure his jellyfish mod was activated, he slammed the Thor on the cancerous growth. The cancer resisted the poison, wiggled as it tried to fight it off, but it lost. The flesh growing on the floor dissolved into carbonate goo.

*Attention, everyone!* said a voice in Felix's mind. *I'm Justin! The panda! My weapon has heart power, and I'm linking everyone's thoughts together, but I can't do it forever! What do we do?*

Felix smiled inwardly. *Thank you, Justin! The ones I assigned, keep working on the laser and the consol. Get those toasters back here!* He sent everyone a flowchart of his idea. Everyone saw and agreed to it. Since Felix was the most leveled up and therefore the most likely to survive, he had to be the one to face Pat.

Joey also had an idea. He aimed his Ridgeback at Pat, who was preparing to launch another cancer attack. Joey activated the telekinesis. Pat flattened against the ceiling, arms splayed out.

Peter raised his kangaroo and fired his laser straight at Pat's heart. It made a clean cut through.

Meanwhile, Felix stamped out the last of the cancerous growths on the floor as a girl with a sheep's member healed some of the cancer victims.

*I can heal them, but it takes time.*

*We'll give you time.*

The girl with the dolphin weapon was in midair, drenching Pat in fire. Pat screamed, but didn't look to be dying. He laughed as he burned. Peter swiped his laser back and forth. It cut off Pat's arms and legs. They fell to the floor and exploded in cancerous masses, which took root on the floor and grew wildly. Felix was on top of them, stamping them out.

He looked up from his battle. Pat was regenerating his limbs. They now looked more like tumors than arms and legs.

*STOP! STOP CUTTING! STOP BURNING! IT'S CANCER! IT DOESN'T KNOW WHEN TO STOP GROWING!*

Everyone had a collective *oh shit* thought, and the two attackers halted.

*I can't hold him forever!* thought Joey.

Pat started to look very much like a lumpy spider; not just his limbs grew, but his whole body.

*How's the progress with the toasters? Have you hacked the system?*

*He was smart. He used a Mac. This will take a while.*

*Damn!*

Felix aimed his weapon at Pat, twisted the ring and released a spray of ice. The ice bored into Pat, pelting him a thousand times. Felix first covered the arms and legs, then the torso and finally the head. Ice built into a glacier.

The growth slowed considerably. But through the thick sheet of ice, Pat grinned down at Felix. The look on his face said, *it's only a matter of time. I am cancer! I'll grow forever!*

The kid with the transmogrifier meerkat aided Felix by changing smaller cancerous lumps into daisies. Felix thanked him mentally, then sprayed more ice on Pat. Pat's grin never waned, and his body cracked the ice as it grew.

*I…can't…hold him…*

*Let him go! Everyone out of the way!*

Joey lowered his weapon. The wielders scattered as the glacier tumbled. It landed flat, didn't bounce. Though the floor cracked in multiple spots, the glacier remained intact.

Joey leaned on his knees, panted. Felix was relieved to see the dolphin girl with her protective shield extended around the whale boy and the control console. The boy with the eagle had rendered the laser invisible, at least for the time being.

Felix kept spraying ice, but the Thor was getting tired. Felix was tired. It didn't matter anyway; he piled on more and more ice, but still it melted underneath. It was only a matter of time before Pat would be able to extend his limbs.

The others sensed Felix's thoughts and braced themselves for the onslaught. They had a new plan: cut Pat's limbs into smaller and smaller pieces so they could be transmogrified into daisies.

Just as Felix expected, the bottom of the ice sheet melted down to the concrete. Pat pushed himself up, threw off the ice sheet and stretched his massive, tentacle-like limbs.

Norman leapt into the air, plunged the Aslan into Pat's shoulder and carved off one of the arms. Pat screamed and thrashed.

*I got it! I got it! Calling the toasters back!*

*Open the ceiling!*

A moment later, the ceiling started to fold down. Pat looked up at it, kicked off with one foot and soared up and out of the lab. He punched a large hole through the warehouse roof and headed for the clouds.

Felix swirled the Thor and gathered the air into a vortex. He channeled some of the air underneath him and rode it up, into the core of the developing tornado.

He soared through the roof of the warehouse. The tornado caught up with Pat, and he tumbled head over heel within it. Clouds were sucked into it. The friction created lightning and thunder inside.

They were now a mile above the city. The toasters began arriving. They flew close to the warehouse and were swept up in the vortex. Felix kept swinging his Thor, gathering up still more air and clouds.

Pat regained control of himself. He flew to the wall of rotating clouds, but it was too thick and it deflected him whenever he tried to break through. He turned around and flew towards Felix.

"I knew you'd be the one!" Pat screamed. "But you can't win now! Labor unions will spread, just as I will spread! Power will return to the people again!"

"Never!" shouted Felix, feeling suddenly patriotic. "Corporation-rule and cheap labor will always triumph over human rights!"

Pat was too close. Felix stopped gathering air and held the Thor at ready. When Pat was in range, Felix swung, slamming him in the chest. Pat cringed as the jellyfish venom coursed through his veins. Basketball sized tumors—poisoned and dead—fell from him.

More toasters were sucked into the tornado and spun around the vortex's walls.

Felix swung the Thor over his head and maintained the tornado while Pat reeled in pain. But the cancer started to regrow. After a moment, the venom wore off and Pat flew against the erratic winds toward Felix

Felix tried to fly away, against the wind...and realized he couldn't fly. He fell into the currents, and straight into Pat's grip. Felix was sure Pat's cancerous penis was gripping him tight, squeezing him. His weapon arm was pinned to his side, useless.

"I was like you once, Felix! But then I grew old and bitter! This is your fate one day, kid!"

Felix struggled to free his weapon arm. A proboscis rose out of Pat's penis, dripping chaotically reproducing cells. It extended, going for Felix's mouth. He struggled and clenched his lips shut.

While Pat had been holding Felix, he hadn't been flying. They collided with the vortex wall and tumbled over each other. The strong currents pushed them apart. His penis lost its grip on Felix and released him. Felix rode the winds out and circled around to the other side.

*ALL THE TOASTERS ARE IN THE VORTEX! NOW, FELIX!*

Felix swung the Thor harder, faster. The walls of the vortex closed in. Tighter. Tighter. A few toasters trapped in the outer wall collided and detonated.

Pat saw this. He cursed and flew again for Felix. Felix swung and swung and SWUNG AND SWUNG AND SWUNG AND—

The twister closed in tighter and tighter and tighter and—

—SWUNG AND SWUNG AND SWUNGSWUNGSWUN-GSWUNG—

The tornado rotated faster. The winds became too strong to fly in any direction; Pat was trapped in the center. The vortex walls compressed. Felix allowed the outer wall to sweep him up towards the mouth of the vortex.

"I'll be back!" Pat screamed. "I swear this isn't over! Cancer never dies! Limited capitalism never dies! I will have my revenge!"

Felix smiled as he ascended. "Sorry. But all you'll get…is your chemo!"

Pat shrieked as the shell of toasters detonated all over him. Thousands of tiny nuclear reactors magnified each other, setting fire to the air. Clouds ignited and smoldered.

The vortex sent Felix careening. He aimed the Thor up against his head and prepared for a rough landing. Felix fell for a full two minutes. He landed squarely on the Thor, which pistoned and absorbed the shock. Felix tipped over and landed on his back in a patch of soft grass. He spread his arms and legs and wheezed for ten minutes.

A window to heaven opened up. The Sacred Horse looked down at him, smiling.

"Excellent catchphrase, warrior."

Felix gave the Sacred Horse the thumbs up. His arm dropped; he lay spread-eagle and wheezed some more.

# * Epilogue *

Thankfully, the boy with giraffe used his deflector powers to shield the city itself from the blast, so other than the warehouse, not a single building was lost.

They dismantled the laser and transmogrified the cooling rod into a harmless bed of flowers. It would have been just daisies, but the meerkat leveled up and gained the ability to create any flower it pleased.

The leftover cancerous masses were exterminated or transmogrified. When the work was over, the wielders gathered inside the empty lab one last time. They compared penises; they compared sacred weapons. An orgy followed. When it was over, they said their goodbyes.

At that moment, a window to heaven opened across the expanse of the concrete ceiling. Looking down at them were the sacred animals, all smiling in their own unique ways. The Sacred Dragon stepped forward.

"We are proud of you all for what you have achieved," he said.

The Sacred Horse then stepped forward. "We have decided to work together now. No longer will we act independently to address threats to life on Earth, and neither should you."

"We are not recollecting your weapons," said the Lion. "Not yet. Other threats have been observed. They're just seedlings now, but if left alone, they will grow too large for even your combined powers to match."

The Sacred Dolphin swam through the air. "If you agree, we shall declare you the Sacred Heroes of Humanity!"

Felix smiled. He raised his Thor high and shouted, "I will!"

In seconds, not a single person's weapon was pointed at the floor. Felix looked back and forth at the army of wielders. They were of one mind. One cause. Indivisible. Forevermore, they would fight for truth, justice and the status quo.

May – August 2010

*Perhaps there was another use for the Thor.*

The Thor (level 1) can be purchased from www.zoofur.com

The Ridgeback (levels 1 – 3) can be purchased from www.bad-dragon.com

All other sacred weapons must be obtained through means not endorsed by the ASPCA.

## ABOUT THE AUTHOR

James Steele lives in Ohio. He does not write vampire romance. He does not write about magic school. In spite of this, he has been published before, in the Magazine of Bizarro Fiction (issue 3), and Anthrozine (issue 18). Others are forthcoming. His blog is: http://daydreamingintext.blogspot.com

# Bizarro books

## CATALOG — SPRING 2010

*Bizarro Books publishes under the following imprints:*

www.rawdogscreamingpress.com

www.eraserheadpress.com

www.afterbirthbooks.com

www.swallowdownpress.com

For all your Bizarro needs visit:

# WWW.BIZARROCENTRAL.COM

Introduce yourselves to the bizarro genre and all of its authors with the Bizarro Starter Kit series. Each volume features short novels and short stories by ten of the leading bizarro authors, designed to give you a perfect sampling of the genre for only $5 plus shipping.

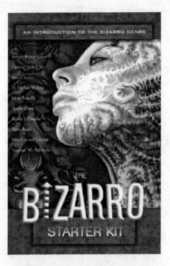

## BB-0X1
## "The Bizarro Starter Kit" (Orange)

Featuring D. Harlan Wilson, Carlton Mellick III, Jeremy Robert Johnson, Kevin L Donihe, Gina Ranalli, Andre Duza, Vincent W. Sakowski, Steve Beard, John Edward Lawson, and Bruce Taylor.

**236 pages   $5**

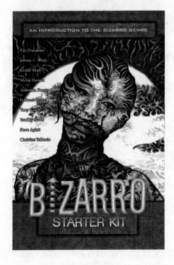

## BB-0X2
## "The Bizarro Starter Kit" (Blue)

Featuring Ray Fracalossy, Jeremy C. Shipp, Jordan Krall, Mykle Hansen, Andersen Prunty, Eckhard Gerdes, Bradley Sands, Steve Aylett, Christian TeBordo, and Tony Rauch.

**244 pages   $5**

BB-001"The Kafka Effekt" D. Harlan Wilson - A collection of forty-four irreal short stories loosely written in the vein of Franz Kafka, with more than a pinch of William S. Burroughs sprinkled on top. **211 pages   $14**

BB-002 "Satan Burger" Carlton Mellick III - The cult novel that put Carlton Mellick III on the map ... Six punks get jobs at a fast food restaurant owned by the devil in a  city violently overpopulated by surreal alien cultures. **236 pages   $14**

BB-003 "Some Things Are Better Left Unplugged" Vincent Sakwoski - Join The Man and his Nemesis, the obese tabby, for a nightmare roller coaster ride into this postmodern fantasy. **152 pages   $10**

BB-004 "Shall We Gather At the Garden?" Kevin L Donihe - Donihe's Debut novel.  Midgets take over the world, The Church of Lionel Richie vs. The Church of the Byrds, plant porn and more! **244 pages   $14**

BB-005 "Razor Wire Pubic Hair" Carlton Mellick III - A genderless humandildo is purchased by a razor dominatrix and brought into her nightmarish world of bizarre sex and mutilation. **176 pages   $11**

BB-006 "Stranger on the Loose" D. Harlan Wilson - The fiction of Wilson's 2nd collection is planted in the soil of normalcy, but what grows out of that soil is a dark, witty, otherworldly jungle... **228 pages   $14**

BB-007 "The Baby Jesus Butt Plug" Carlton Mellick III - Using clones of the Baby Jesus for anal sex will be the hip sex fetish of the future. **92 pages   $10**

BB-008 "Fishyfleshed" Carlton Mellick III - The world of the past is an illogical flatland lacking in dimension and color, a sick-scape of crispy squid people wandering the desert for no apparent reason. **260 pages   $14**

BB-009 **"Dead Bitch Army" Andre Duza** - Step into a world filled with racist teenagers, cannibals, 100 warped Uncle Sams, automobiles with razor-sharp teeth, living graffiti, and a pissed-off zombie bitch out for revenge. **344 pages $16**

BB-010 **"The Menstruating Mall" Carlton Mellick III** - "The Breakfast Club meets Chopping Mall as directed by David Lynch." - Brian Keene **212 pages $12**

BB-011 **"Angel Dust Apocalypse" Jeremy Robert Johnson** - Meth-heads, man-made monsters, and murderous Neo-Nazis. "Seriously amazing short stories..." - Chuck Palahniuk, author of Fight Club **184 pages $11**

BB-012 **"Ocean of Lard" Kevin L Donihe / Carlton Mellick III** - A parody of those old Choose Your Own Adventure kid's books about some very odd pirates sailing on a sea made of animal fat. **176 pages $12**

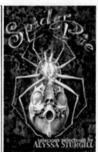

BB-013 **"Last Burn in Hell" John Edward Lawson** - From his lurid angst-affair with a lesbian music diva to his ascendance as unlikely pop icon the one constant for Kenrick Brimley, official state prison gigolo, is he's got no clue what he's doing. **172 pages $14**

BB-014 **"Tangerinephant" Kevin Dole 2** - TV-obsessed aliens have abducted Michael Tangerinephant in this bizarro combination of science fiction, satire, and surrealism. **164 pages $11**

BB-015 **"Foop!" Chris Genoa** - Strange happenings are going on at Dactyl, Inc, the world's first and only time travel tourism company.

"A surreal pie in the face!" - Christopher Moore **300 pages $14**

BB-016 **"Spider Pie" Alyssa Sturgill** - A one-way trip down a rabbit hole inhabited by sexual deviants and friendly monsters, fairytale beginnings and hideous endings. **104 pages $11**

**BB-017 "The Unauthorized Woman" Efrem Emerson** - Enter the world of the inner freak, a landscape populated by the pre-dead and morticioners, by cockroaches and 300-lb robots. **104 pages $11**

**BB-018 "Fugue XXIX" Forrest Aguirre** - Tales from the fringe of speculative literary fiction where innovative minds dream up the future's uncharted territories while mining forgotten treasures of the past. **220 pages $16**

**BB-019 "Pocket Full of Loose Razorblades" John Edward Lawson** - A collection of dark bizarro stories. From a giant rectum to a foot-fungus factory to a girl with a biforked tongue. **190 pages $13**

**BB-020 "Punk Land" Carlton Mellick III** - In the punk version of Heaven, the anarchist utopia is threatened by corporate fascism and only Goblin, Mortician's sperm, and a blue-mohawked female assassin named Shark Girl can stop them. **284 pages $15**

**BB-021"Pseudo-City" D. Harlan Wilson** - Pseudo-City exposes what waits in the bathroom stall, under the manhole cover and in the corporate boardroom, all in a way that can only be described as mind-bogglingly irreal. **220 pages $16**

**BB-022 "Kafka's Uncle and Other Strange Tales" Bruce Taylor** - Anslenot and his giant tarantula (tormentor? fri-end?) wander a desecrated world in this novel and collection of stories from Mr. Magic Realism Himself. **348 pages $17**

**BB-023 "Sex and Death In Television Town" Carlton Mellick III** - In the old west, a gang of hermaphrodite gunslingers take refuge from a demon plague in Telos: a town where its citizens have televisions instead of heads. **184 pages $12**

**BB-024 "It Came From Below The Belt" Bradley Sands** - What can Grover Goldstein do when his severed, sentient penis forces him to return to high school and help it win the presidential election? **204 pages $13**

BB-025 **"Sick: An Anthology of Illness" John Lawson, editor** - These Sick stories are horrendous and hilarious dissections of creative minds on the scalpel's edge. **296 pages $16**

BB-026 **"Tempting Disaster" John Lawson, editor** - A shocking and alluring anthology from the fringe that examines our culture's obsession with taboos. **260 pages $16**

BB-027 **"Siren Promised" Jeremy Robert Johnson & Alan M Clark** - Nominated for the Bram Stoker Award. A potent mix of bad drugs, bad dreams, brutal bad guys, and surreal/incredible art by Alan M. Clark. **190 pages $13**

BB-028 **"Chemical Gardens" Gina Ranalli** - Ro and punk band Green is the Enemy find Kreepkins, a surfer-dude warlock, a vengeful demon, and a Metal Priestess in their way as they try to escape an underground nightmare. **188 pages $13**

BB-029 **"Jesus Freaks" Andre Duza** - For God so loved the world that he gave his only two begotten sons... and a few million zombies. **400 pages $16**

BB-030 **"Grape City" Kevin L. Donihe** - More Donihe-style comedic bizarro about a demon named Charles who is forced to work a minimum wage job on Earth after Hell goes out of business. **108 pages $10**

BB-031 **"Sea of the Patchwork Cats" Carlton Mellick III** - A quiet dreamlike tale set in the ashes of the human race. For Mellick enthusiasts who also adore The Twilight Zone. **112 pages $10**

BB-032 **"Extinction Journals" Jeremy Robert Johnson** - An uncanny voyage across a newly nuclear America where one man must confront the problems associated with loneliness, insane dieties, radiation, love, and an ever-evolving cockroach suit with a mind of its own. **104 pages $10**

BB-033 **"Meat Puppet Cabaret" Steve Beard** - At last! The secret connection between Jack the Ripper and Princess Diana's death revealed! **240 pages $16 / $30**

BB-034 **"The Greatest Fucking Moment in Sports" Kevin L. Donihe** - In the tradition of the surreal anti-sitcom Get A Life comes a tale of triumph and agape love from the master of comedic bizarro. **108 pages $10**

BB-035 **"The Troublesome Amputee" John Edward Lawson** - Disturbing verse from a man who truly believes nothing is sacred and intends to prove it. **104 pages $9**

BB-036 **"Deity" Vic Mudd** - God (who doesn't like to be called "God") comes down to a typical, suburban, Ohio family for a little vacation—but it doesn't turn out to be as relaxing as He had hoped it would be... **168 pages $12**

BB-037 **"The Haunted Vagina" Carlton Mellick III** - It's difficult to love a woman whose vagina is a gateway to the world of the dead. **132 pages $10**

BB-038 **"Tales from the Vinegar Wasteland" Ray Fracalossy** - Witness: a man is slowly losing his face, a neighbor who periodically screams out for no apparent reason, and a house with a room that doesn't actually exist. **240 pages $14**

BB-039 **"Suicide Girls in the Afterlife" Gina Ranalli** - After Pogue commits suicide, she unexpectedly finds herself an unwilling "guest" at a hotel in the Afterlife, where she meets a group of bizarre characters, including a goth Satan, a hippie Jesus, and an alien-human hybrid. **100 pages $9**

BB-040 **"And Your Point Is?" Steve Aylett** - In this follow-up to LINT multiple authors provide critical commentary and essays about Jeff Lint's mind-bending literature. **104 pages $11**

BB-041 **"Not Quite One of the Boys"  Vincent Sakowski** - While drug-dealer Maxi drinks with Dante in purgatory, God and Satan play a little tri-level chess and do a little bargaining over his business partner, Vinnie, who is still left on earth. **220 pages  $14**

BB-042 **"Teeth and Tongue Landscape" Carlton Mellick III** - On a planet made out of meat, a socially-obsessive monophobic man tries to find his place amongst the strange creatures and communities that he comes across. **110  pages  $10**

BB-043 **"War Slut"  Carlton Mellick III** - Part "1984," part "Waiting for Godot," and part action horror video game adaptation of John Carpenter's "The Thing." **116 pages  $10**

BB-044 **"All Encompassing Trip"  Nicole Del Sesto** - In a world where coffee is no longer available, the only television shows are reality TV re-runs, and the animals are talking back, Nikki, Amber and a singing Coyote in a do-rag are out to restore the light  **308 pages  $15**

BB-045 **"Dr. Identity"  D. Harlan Wilson** - Follow the Dystopian Duo on a killing spree of epic proportions through the irreal postcapitalist city of Bliptown where time ticks sideways, artificial Bug-Eyed Monsters punish citizens for consumer-capitalist lethargy, and ultraviolence is as essential as a daily multivitamin. **208 pages  $15**

BB-046 **"The Million-Year Centipede"  Eckhard Gerdes** - Wakelin, frontman for 'The Hinge,' wrote a poem so prophetic that to ignore it dooms a person to drown in blood. **130 pages  $12**

BB-047 **"Sausagey Santa"  Carlton Mellick III** - A bizarro Christmas tale featuring Santa as a piratey mutant with a body made of sausages. 124 pages  $10

BB-048 **"Misadventures in a Thumbnail Universe" Vincent Sakowski** - Dive deep into the surreal and satirical realms of neo-classical Blender Fiction, filled with television shoes and flesh-filled skies. **120 pages  $10**

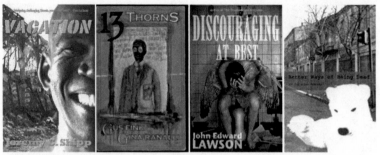

BB-049 **"Vacation" Jeremy C. Shipp** - Blueblood Bernard Johnson leaved his boring life behind to go on The Vacation, a year-long corporate sponsored odyssey. But instead of seeing the world, Bernard is captured by terrorists, becomes a key figure in secret drug wars, and, worse, doesn't once miss his secure American Dream. **160 pages $14**

BB-051 **"13 Thorns" Gina Ranalli** - Thirteen tales of twisted, bizarro horror. **240 pages $13**

BB-050 **"Discouraging at Best" John Edward Lawson** - A collection where the absurdity of the mundane expands exponentially creating a tidal wave that sweeps reason away. For those who enjoy satire, bizarro, or a good old-fashioned slap to the senses. **208 pages $15**

BB-052 **"Better Ways of Being Dead" Christian TeBordo** - In this class, the students have to keep one palm down on the table at all times, and listen to lectures about a panda who speaks Chinese. **216 pages $14**

BB-053 **"Ballad of a Slow Poisoner" Andrew Goldfarb** Millford Mutterwurst sat down on a Tuesday to take his afternoon tea, and made the unpleasant discovery that his elbows were becoming flatter. **128 pages $10**

BB-054 **"Wall of Kiss" Gina Ranalli** - A woman... A wall... Sometimes love blooms in the strangest of places. **108 pages $9**

BB-055 **"HELP! A Bear is Eating Me" Mykle Hansen** - The bizarro, heartwarming, magical tale of poor planning, hubris and severe blood loss... **150 pages $11**

BB-056 **"Piecemeal June" Jordan Krall** - A man falls in love with a living sex doll, but with love comes danger when her creator comes after her with crab-squid assassins. **90 pages $9**

BB-057 **"Laredo" Tony Rauch** - Dreamlike, surreal stories by Tony Rauch. **180 pages $12**

BB-058 **"The Overwhelming Urge" Andersen Prunty** - A collection of bizarro tales by Andersen Prunty. **150 pages $11**

BB-059 **"Adolf in Wonderland" Carlton Mellick III** - A dreamlike adventure that takes a young descendant of Adolf Hitler's design and sends him down the rabbit hole into a world of imperfection and disorder. **180 pages $11**

BB-060 **"Super Cell Anemia" Duncan B. Barlow** - "Unrelentingly bizarre and mysterious, unsettling in all the right ways..." - Brian Evenson. **180 pages $12**

BB-061 **"Ultra Fuckers" Carlton Mellick III** - Absurdist suburban horror about a couple who enter an upper middle class gated community but can't find their way out. **108 pages $9**

BB-062 **"House of Houses" Kevin L. Donihe** - An odd man wants to marry his house. Unfortunately, all of the houses in the world collapse at the same time in the Great House Holocaust. Now he must travel to House Heaven to find his departed fiancee. **172 pages $11**

BB-063 **"Necro Sex Machine" Andre Duza** - The Dead Bitch returns in this follow-up to the bizarro zombie epic Dead Bitch Army. **400 pages $16**

BB-064 **"Squid Pulp Blues" Jordan Krall** - In these three bizarro-noir novellas, the reader is thrown into a world of murderers, drugs made from squid parts, deformed gun-toting veterans, and a mischievous apocalyptic donkey. **204 pages $12**

BB-065 **"Jack and Mr. Grin" Andersen Prunty** - "When Mr. Grin calls you can hear a smile in his voice. Not a warm and friendly smile, but the kind that seizes your spine in fear. You don't need to pay your phone bill to hear it. That smile is in every line of Prunty's prose." - Tom Bradley. **208 pages $12**

BB-066 **"Cybernetrix" Carlton Mellick III** - What would you do if your normal everyday world was slowly mutating into the video game world from Tron? **212 pages $12**

BB-067 **"Lemur" Tom Bradley** - Spencer Sproul is a would-be serial-killing bus boy who can't manage to murder, injure, or even scare anybody. However, there are other ways to do damage to far more people and do it legally... **120 pages $12**

BB-068 **"Cocoon of Terror" Jason Earls** - Decapitated corpses...a sculpture of terror...Zelian's masterpiece, his Cocoon of Terror, will trigger a supernatural disaster for everyone on Earth. **196 pages $14**

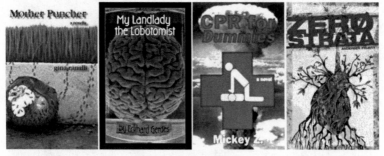

BB-069 **"Mother Puncher" Gina Ranalli** - The world has become tragically over-populated and now the government strongly opposes procreation. Ed is employed by the government as a mother-puncher. He doesn't relish his job, but he knows it has to be done and he knows he's the best one to do it. **120 pages $9**

BB-070 **"My Landlady the Lobotomist" Eckhard Gerdes** - The brains of past tenants line the shelves of my boarding house, soaking in a mysterious elixir. One more slip-up and the landlady might just add my frontal lobe to her collection. **116 pages $12**

BB-071 **"CPR for Dummies" Mickey Z.** - This hilarious freakshow at the world's end is the fragmented, sobering debut novel by acclaimed nonfiction author Mickey Z. **216 pages $14**

BB-072 **"Zerostrata" Andersen Prunty** - Hansel Nothing lives in a tree house, suffers from memory loss, has a very eccentric family, and falls in love with a woman who runs naked through the woods every night. **144 pages $11**

BB-073 **"The Egg Man" Carlton Mellick III** - It is a world where humans reproduce like insects. Children are the property of corporations, and having an enormous ten-foot brain implanted into your skull is a grotesque sexual fetish. Mellick's industrial urban dystopia is one of his darkest and grittiest to date. **184 pages $11**

BB-074 **"Shark Hunting in Paradise Garden" Cameron Pierce** - A group of strange humanoid religious fanatics travel back in time to the Garden of Eden to discover it is invested with hundreds of giant flying maneating sharks. **150 pages $10**

BB-075 **"Apeshit" Carlton Mellick III** - Friday the 13th meets Visitor Q. Six hipster teens go to a cabin in the woods inhabited by a deformed killer. An incredibly fucked-up parody of B-horror movies with a bizarro slant. **192 pages $12**

BB-076 **"Rampaging Fuckers of Everything on the Crazy Shitting Planet At smosphere" Mykle Hansen** - 3 bizarro satires. Monster Cocks, Journey to the Center of Agnes Cuddlebottom, and Crazy Shitting Planet. **228 pages $12**

BB-077 **"The Kissing Bug" Daniel Scott Buck** - In the tradition of Roald Dahl, Tim Burton, and Edward Gorey, comes this bizarro anti-war children's story about a bohemian conenose kissing bug who falls in love with a human woman. **116 pages $10**

BB-078 **"MachoPoni" Lotus Rose** - It's My Little Pony... *Bizarro* style! A long time ago Poniworld was split in two. On one side of the Jagged Line is the Pastel Kingdom, a magical land of music, parties, and positivity. On the other side of the Jagged Line is Dark Kingdom inhabited by an army of undead ponies. **148 pages $11**

BB-079 **"The Faggiest Vampire" Carlton Mellick III** - A Roald Dahl-esque children's story about two faggy vampires who partake in a mustache competition to find out which one is truly the faggiest. **104 pages $10**

BB-080 **"Sky Tongues" Gina Ranalli** - The autobiography of Sky Tongues, the biracial hermaphrodite actress with tongues for fingers. Follow her strange life story as she rises from freak to fame. **204 pages $12**

BB-081 **"Washer Mouth" Kevin L. Donihe** - A washing machine becomes human and pursues his dream of meeting his favorite soap opera star. **244 pages $11**

BB-082 **"Shatnerquake" Jeff Burk** - All of the characters ever played by William Shatner are suddenly sucked into our world. Their mission: hunt down and destroy the real William Shatner. **100 pages $10**

BB-083 **"The Cannibals of Candyland" Carlton Mellick III** - There exists a race of cannibals that are made of candy. They live in an underground world made out of candy. One man has dedicated his life to killing them all. **170 pages $11**

BB-084 **"Slub Glub in the Weird World of the Weeping Willows"**
**Andrew Goldfarb** - The charming tale of a blue glob named Slub Glub who helps the weeping willows whose tears are flooding the earth. There are also hyenas, ghosts, and a voodoo priest **100 pages $10**

BB-085 **"Super Fetus" Adam Pepper** - Try to abort this fetus and he'll kick your ass! **104 pages $10**

BB-086 **"Fistful of Feet" Jordan Krall** - A bizarro tribute to spaghetti westerns, featuring Cthulhu-worshipping Indians, a woman with four feet, a crazed gunman who is obsessed with sucking on candy, Syphilis-ridden mutants, sexually transmitted tattoos, and a house devoted to the freakiest fetishes. **228 pages $12**

BB-087 **"Ass Goblins of Auschwitz" Cameron Pierce** - It's Monty Python meets Nazi exploitation in a surreal nightmare as can only be imagined by Bizarro author Cameron Pierce. **104 pages $10**

BB-088 **"Silent Weapons for Quiet Wars" Cody Goodfellow** - "This is high-end psychological surrealist horror meets bottom-feeding low-life crime in a techno-thrilling science fiction world full of Lovecraft and magic..." -John Skipp **212 pages $12**

**BB-089 "Warrior Wolf Women of the Wasteland" Carlton Mellick III**
Road Warrior Werewolves versus McDonaldland Mutants...post-apocalyptic fiction has never been quite like this. **316 pages $13**

**BB-090 "Cursed" Jeremy C Shipp** - The story of a group of characters who believe they are cursed and attempt to figure out who cursed them and why. A tale of stylish absurdism and suspenseful horror. **218 pages $15**

**BB-091 "Super Giant Monster Time" Jeff Burk** - A tribute to choose your own adventures and Godzilla movies. Will you escape the giant monsters that are rampaging the fuck out of your city and shit? Or will you join the mob of alien-controlled punk rockers causing chaos in the streets? What happens next depends on you. **188 pages $12**

**BB-092 "Perfect Union" Cody Goodfellow** - "Cronenberg's THE FLY on a grand scale: human/insect gene-spliced body horror, where the human hive politics are as shocking as the gore." -John Skipp. **272 pages $13**

**BB-093 "Sunset with a Beard" Carlton Mellick III** - 14 stories of surreal science fiction. **200 pages $12**

**BB-094 "My Fake War" Andersen Prunty** - The absurd tale of an unlikely soldier forced to fight a war that, quite possibly, does not exist. It's Rambo meets Waiting for Godot in this subversive satire of American values and the scope of the human imagination. **128 pages $11**

**BB-095 "Lost in Cat Brain Land" Cameron Pierce** - Sad stories from a surreal world. A fascist mustache, the ghost of Franz Kafka, a desert inside a dead cat. Primordial entities mourn the death of their child. The desperate serve tea to mysterious creatures. A hopeless romantic falls in love with a pterodactyl. And much more. **152 pages $11**

**BB-096 "The Kobold Wizard's Dildo of Enlightenment +2" Carlton Mellick III** - A Dungeons and Dragons parody about a group of people who learn they are only made up characters in an AD&D campaign and must find a way to resist their nerdy teenaged players and retarded dungeon master in order to survive. 232 **pages $12**

BB-097 **"My Heart Said No, but the Camera Crew Said Yes!" Bradley Sands** - A collection of short stories that are crammed with the delightfully odd and the scurrilously silly. **140 pages $13**

BB-098 **"A Hundred Horrible Sorrows of Ogner Stump" Andrew Goldfarb** - Goldfarb's acclaimed comic series. A magical and weird journey into the horrors of everyday life. **164 pages $11**

BB-099 **"Pickled Apocalypse of Pancake Island" Cameron Pierce** A demented fairy tale about a pickle, a pancake, and the apocalypse. **102 pages $8**

BB-100 **"Slag Attack" Andersen Prunty** - Slag Attack features four visceral, noir stories about the living, crawling apocalypse. A slag is what survivors are calling the slug-like maggots raining from the sky, burrowing inside people, and hollowing out their flesh and their sanity. **148 pages $11**

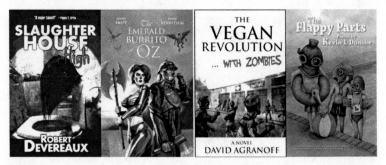

BB-101 **"Slaughterhouse High" Robert Devereaux** - A place where schools are built with secret passageways, rebellious teens get zippers installed in their mouths and genitals, and once a year, on that special night, one couple is slaughtered and the bits of their bodies are kept as souvenirs. **304 pages $13**

BB-102 **"The Emerald Burrito of Oz" John Skipp & Marc Levinthal** OZ IS REAL! Magic is real! The gate is really in Kansas! And America is finally allowing Earth tourists to visit this weird-ass, mysterious land. But when Gene of Los Angeles heads off for summer vacation in the Emerald City, little does he know that a war is brewing...a war that could destroy both worlds. **280 pages $13**

BB-103 **"The Vegan Revolution... with Zombies" David Agranoff** When there's no more meat in hell, the vegans will walk the earth. **160 pages $11**

BB-104 **"The Flappy Parts" Kevin L Donihe** - Poems about bunnies, LSD, and police abuse. You know, things that matter. 132 **pages $11**

# ORDER FORM

| TITLES | QTY | PRICE | TOTAL |
|--------|-----|-------|-------|
|        |     |       |       |
|        |     |       |       |
|        |     |       |       |
|        |     |       |       |
|        |     |       |       |
|        |     |       |       |
|        |     |       |       |
|        |     |       |       |
|        |     |       |       |
|        |     |       |       |
|        |     |       |       |
|        |     |       |       |
|        |     |       |       |
|        |     |       |       |
|        |     |       |       |
|        |     |       |       |

Please make checks and moneyorders payable to ROSE O'KEEFE / BIZARRO BOOKS in U.S. funds only. Please don't send bad checks! Allow 2-6 weeks for delivery. International orders may take longer. If you'd like to pay online via PAYPAL.COM, send payments to publisher@eraserheadpress.com.

**SHIPPING:** US ORDERS - $2 for the first book, $1 for each additional book. For priority shipping, add an additional $4. INT'L ORDERS - $5 for the first book, $3 for each additional book. Add an additional $5 per book for global priority shipping.

**Send payment to:**

**BIZARRO BOOKS**
   **C/O Rose O'Keefe**
   **205 NE Bryant**
   **Portland, OR 97211**

Address

City                        State      Zip

Email                       Phone